|
a ... **y partners**

Officer:	John Forrester
Age:	34
K-9 Partner:	Samson the German Shepherd
Assignment:	Protect his next-door neighbor from the person who keeps breaking into her newly inherited house.

Officer:	Dylan Ralsey
Age:	32
K-9 Partner:	Tico the Belgian Malinois
Assignment:	Keep a diplomat's daughter safe from the man who killed her father.

Aside from her faith and her family, there's not much **Shirlee McCoy** enjoys more than a good book! When she's not teaching or chauffeuring her five kids, she can usually be found plotting her next Love Inspired Suspense story or wandering around the beautiful Inland Northwest in search of inspiration. Shirlee loves to hear from readers. Drop her a line at shirlee@shirleemccoy.com and visit her website at shirleemccoy.com.

Lenora Worth writes award-winning romance and romantic suspense. Three of her books finaled in the ACFW Carol Awards, and her Love Inspired Suspense novel *Body of Evidence* became a *New York Times* bestseller. Her novella in *Mistletoe Kisses* made her a *USA TODAY* bestselling author. With sixty books published and millions in print, she goes on adventures with her retired husband, Don, and enjoys reading, baking and shopping...especially shoe shopping.

CAPITOL
K-9 UNIT
CHRISTMAS

SHIRLEE McCOY
LENORA WORTH

HARLEQUIN® LOVE INSPIRED® SUSPENSE

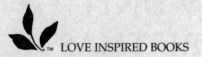 **LOVE INSPIRED BOOKS**

Recycling programs
for this product may
not exist in your area.

ISBN-13: 978-0-373-44702-2

Capitol K-9 Unit Christmas

Copyright © 2015 by Harlequin Books S.A.

Thanks and acknowledgment to Shirlee McCoy and Lenora Worth
for their participation in the Capitol K-9 Unit series.

Protecting Virginia
Copyright © 2015 by Harlequin Books S.A.

Guarding Abigail
Copyright © 2015 by Harlequin Books S.A.

www.Harlequin.com

Printed in U.S.A.

CONTENTS

PROTECTING VIRGINIA   9
Shirlee McCoy

GUARDING ABIGAIL   111
Lenora Worth

PROTECTING VIRGINIA

Shirlee McCoy

To my Monday morning breakfast buddy.
Thanks for always making time for me, Ms. Marge!

You will keep in perfect peace all who trust in you,
all whose thoughts are fixed on you.
–*Isaiah* 26:3

ONE

The house looked exactly the way Virginia Johnson remembered it—a hulking Victorian with a wraparound porch and gingerbread trim. The once-lush lawn had died, the wrought iron fence that separated the yard from the sidewalk was leaning inward, but the ancient oak still stood at the right corner of the property, a tire swing hanging listlessly from its branches.

Even with dead grass and darkened windows, the property was impressive, the beautiful details of the house highlighted by bright winter sun. Most people would have been thrilled to inherit a place like this.

Virginia was horrified.

She walked up the driveway, her throat tight with a hundred memories that she'd rather forget, her hand clamped around the key that had come in the mail three weeks ago. It had been in a package with a letter from a lawyer who'd been trying to reach her for two months, a check for more money than she knew what to do with and the deed to the house.

She hadn't wanted any of it.

She'd torn up the check, tossed the deed and the key in the trash. Would have gone on with her life and pretended her grandmother-in-law, Laurel, hadn't left her everything the Johnson family owned. Except that kids were nosy, and Virginia's job as assistant housemother at All Our Kids Foster Home meant that she lived and worked with children all the time.

Most days, she loved her job. The day little Tommy Benson had taken the letter, torn-up check, key and deed out of the trashcan and delivered them to Virginia's boss, Cassie McCord, Virginia found herself wishing that she worked in a tiny little cubicle in a sales department somewhere. Because Cassie wasn't one to let things go. She couldn't understand why Virginia would let a beautiful home rot.

If you don't want it, why not sell it? she'd asked. *You haven't had any time off in three years. Take a couple of weeks off, contact an auction house. Have them auction what you don't want to keep, then you can put the house on the market. Imagine what you could do with the money, how many kids you could help.*

The last part had been the catalyst that had changed Virginia's mind. She *could* do a lot with the money from the estate. She could open another foster home. She could help hundreds of children.

And maybe…just maybe…going back to the place where she'd nearly died, the place where every one of her dreams had turned into a nightmare, would help her conquer the anxiety and fear that seemed to have taken over her life.

If it didn't kill her first.

She shivered, the late November air cutting through her coat and chilling her to the bone. Her legs felt stiff as she walked up the porch steps. It had been eight years since she'd seen the property, but it hadn't changed much. The door was still brick red, the porch and railing crisp white. The flowered welcome mat had been replaced by a plain black one. If she lifted it, would she see blood-stains on the porch boards?

She gagged at the thought, her hand shaking as she shoved the key in the lock. The door swung open before she could turn the knob, and she jumped back, startled, afraid.

Of what? her rational self whispered. *He's not here. Won't ever be here again.*

She stepped inside, closed the door behind her, stood there in the foyer the way she had the very first time she'd seen the property. Kevin had been beside her, proud of what he had to offer the woman he'd said he loved.

She gagged again, the scent of blood filling her nose. Only there was no blood. Not on the foyer floor. Not on the cream-colored walls. Someone had washed things down, painted them over, hidden the horror that had happened in a house that should have been filled with love.

"Just get it over with," she muttered, forcing herself to walk down the long hall and into the kitchen. She'd start her itemized list there.

The house had been in the Johnson family for five generations. It was filled to the brim with things that had been passed down from one family member to the next. The line had ended with Kevin's death. There were probably cousins of cousins somewhere, and Virginia wished her grandmother-in-law had found one of them to hand the property and the money over to. Instead, Laurel had passed the property on to Virginia. A guilt offering? It didn't matter. All Virginia wanted to do was get rid of it as quickly as possible.

A floorboard above her head creaked, and she froze, her hand on an old pitcher and bowl set that dated back to the nineteenth century.

"The house settling," she said aloud, the words echoing hollowly in the quiet room.

She knew the old house well, had lived in it for two long years. It creaked. It groaned. It protested its age loudly. Especially in the winter. She knew it, but she was still terrified, her hand shaking as she set the pitcher down.

The floor creaked again, and every fear that haunted her dreams, every terror that woke her from sound sleep, filled her mind. She inhaled. Exhaled. Told herself that she had nothing to be afraid of.

Another board creaked. It sounded like someone walking through the upstairs hallway, heading toward the servants' stairs. *The stairs that led straight down into the kitchen.*

The door to the stairwell was closed, the old crystal doorknob glinting in the overhead light. She cocked her head to the side and listened to what sounded like the landing at the top of the stairs groaning. Her imagination. It had to be.

She opened the door, because she was tired of always being afraid, always jumping at shadows, always panicking. The stairwell was narrow and dark, the air musty. She glanced up, expecting to see the other door, the one that led into the upstairs hallway.

A man stood on the landing. Tall. Gaunt. Hazel eyes and light brown hair.

"Kevin," she breathed, because he looked so much like her husband had that her heart nearly stopped.

He blinked, smiled a smile that made her skin crawl.

"Ginny," he murmured, and that was all she needed to hear.

She ran to the back door and fumbled with the bolt, sure she heard his footsteps on the stairs, his feet padding on the tile behind her.

She didn't look. Couldn't look.

The bolt slid free, and she yanked the door open, sprinted outside.

"Ginny!" the man called, as she jumped off the porch stairs and raced toward the back edge of the property. "Is this the way you treat a man who gave you everything?"

She screamed, the sound ripping from her throat, screaming again as footsteps pounded behind her.

She made it to the hedge that separated the Johnson property from the one behind it and plunged through winter-dry foliage, branches snagging her hair, ripping at her skin.

Was he behind her? His hand reaching to drag her back?

Impossible! Kevin had died eight years ago!

But someone was there, someone was following.

She shoved through the remainder of the hedge, ran into the open, and he was there. Standing in front of her, his broad form backlit by sunlight, his face hidden in shadows.

She pivoted away, screaming again and again.

He snagged her coat, pulled her backward, and she knew that every nightmare she'd ever had, every horrible memory she'd tried to forget had finally come for her.

The woman was hysterical. No doubt about that. Terrified, too. The last thing Capitol K-9 police officer John Forrester wanted to do was scare her more, but he couldn't let her go. She was obviously running from something or someone, and he didn't want her to run right back into whatever danger she'd fled.

"Calm down," he said, tugging her back another step. "I'm not going to hurt you."

She whirled around, took a swing at his head, her fist just missing his nose.

Beside him his K-9 partner, Samson, growled.

That seemed to get her attention.

She froze, her eyes wide as her gaze dropped to the German shepherd. Samson had subsided, his dark eyes locked on Virginia, his muscles relaxed. Obviously, he didn't see the woman as too much of a threat.

"He's not going to hurt you, either," John assured the woman.

She didn't look convinced, but she wasn't screaming any longer.

"That wasn't you in the house," she said as if that made perfect sense.

"What house?" he asked, eyeing the hedge she'd just torn through. The property on the other side of it had been empty for longer than John had been renting the Hendersons' garage apartment. According to his landlords, the elderly woman who owned the house had moved to an assisted-living facility over a year ago.

"Laurel's," the woman said, her hand trembling as she tucked a strand of light brown hair behind her ear. She looked vaguely familiar, her soft blue eyes sparking a memory that he couldn't quite catch hold of.

"Laurel is your friend?" he prodded, anxious to figure out what was going on and get back to his day off.

"My husband's grandmother. She left me the house, so I guess it's actually mine," she corrected herself.

"And you think someone was in there?"

"Someone *was* in there. I saw him."

"Your husband maybe?"

"My husband," she said, every word brittle and sharp, "is dead."

"I'm sorry."

She didn't respond, just fumbled in her pocket and pulled out a cell phone. "I need to call the police."

"I can check things out for you," he offered, because

he was there, and because if someone was in the house, the guy would be gone long before the police arrived.

"I don't think that would be safe," she said, worrying her lower lip, her finger hovering over the 9 on her phone. "He could have a weapon or—"

"I'm a police officer," he interrupted. "I work for Capitol K-9."

She looked up, her gaze sharp. "Then you know Gavin McCord."

The comment brought back the memory he'd been searching for. Captain Gavin McCord's wedding. His bride and her entourage of foster kids, the quiet woman who'd been with them. He hadn't paid all that much attention to her. She'd been pretty enough, her hair swept into some elaborate style, her dress understated, her shoes sturdy. Nothing showy about her. They might have been introduced. He couldn't remember. He'd been too busy thinking about getting food from the buffet.

"You're Cassie's friend," he said, pulling Samson's lead from his pocket and attaching it to the shepherd's collar.

"Yes. Virginia Johnson. Cassie and I work together at All Our Kids." She glanced at the hedge again, tucking another stray strand of hair behind her ear. Her nervous energy made him antsy. He didn't much like sitting idle when he could be doing something, and right at that moment, he and Samson could be searching for whomever she'd seen.

"Tell you what, Virginia," he said. "Go ahead and call the police while I look around. If there's someone in the house, we're giving him way too much time to get away."

"I hope he does get away," she muttered.

"You want him coming back?" he asked, and she flinched.

"No, but I don't want you killed, either, Officer—"

"John Forrester. Stay here. I'll be back soon."

"I'm not waiting out here by myself," she said, moving in behind him as he made his way to the shrubs.

"Then wait at my place." He shoved the keys into her hands, pointing her toward the external staircase that led to his second-floor garage apartment.

"But—"

"Find!" he said, commanding Samson to move forward.

The Shepherd took off, lunging through the shrubs and out into a pristine yard, nose to the ground, body relaxed. He was trained in apprehension and protection. He knew how to track a suspect, corner him and disarm him if necessary.

He was also good at sensing danger, at knowing when someone was around who didn't belong. Right now, he was focused on a scent trail. Probably Virginia's.

John followed as Samson beelined across the lawn and headed straight toward the large Victorian. The Shepherd bounded up the porch stairs, and stopped at a door. Cracked open, a little wedge of light visible beyond, it looked as if it opened into a kitchen.

"Hold!" he commanded and Samson settled onto his haunches, eyes trained on the door.

John nudged it open, peering into an empty kitchen.

"Find," he commanded, and Samson trotted into the room.

The house lay silent, the air thick with something that made the hair on the back of John's neck stand on end. He'd been in enough dangerous situations to know when he was walking into trouble. He could feel it like a cold breeze brushing against his skin.

Samson sensed it, too. His scruff bristled, his body language changing. No longer relaxed, he sniffed the air and moved toward a doorway to their left. Beyond it, a staircase wound its way to the second floor.

Samson charged up, his well-muscled body moving silently. John moved with him. In sync with the Shepherd's loping gait, muscles tense, every nerve alert, he jogged onto the second-floor landing and into a wide hallway. Seven doors. All closed. Another staircase that led downstairs.

Samson growled, the deep low warning seeming to echo through the hallway.

"Police!" John shouted. "Come on out or I'll send my dog to find you."

There was a flurry of movement below. Fabric rustling, footsteps pounding.

Samson barked, yanking at the lead, tugging John into a full-out run.

A door creaked open as they raced downstairs and into a large foyer.

The front door?

Samson veered away from it, pulling John through the foyer into an old-fashioned parlor.

Cold air filled the room, swirling in from an open door that emptied onto a wraparound porch.

"Find!" John commanded, and Samson raced through the open doorway and out into the crisp winter day, his well-muscled body tense with anticipation.

Someone had been in the house. There was no doubt about that. What he was doing there was something John had every intention of finding out.

He ran down porch steps, Samson bounding in front of him. No hesitation. The dog had the scent, and he'd follow it until they found their quarry. Once he did, the guy was going to be very sorry he'd picked that house.

TWO

Virginia didn't know what to do.

That was going to be a problem, because standing in the middle of some guy's yard, waiting while he searched her house for a dead man? That was nuts.

Yet that was exactly what Virginia was doing.

She'd called the police.

She knew they were on the way.

She could have gone inside the garage apartment like Officer Forrester had suggested, but she was frozen with fear, so afraid that she'd move the wrong way, head the wrong direction, make the wrong choice, that she wasn't doing anything at all.

"Snap out of it," she muttered, and the words seemed to break terror's hold.

She could breathe again, think again.

And what she was thinking was that she needed to meet the police and explain what she'd seen. Crazy as it might sound to them, Kevin had been in that house. Or someone who'd looked an awful lot like him, because there was no way the man could have actually been her husband. She'd seen Kevin's gravesite. She'd read the inscription that his grandmother had had carved on the marble stone: *Beloved son. Beloved husband.* Virginia had wanted to scratch those words out, just leave his birth and death dates.

Of course, she hadn't.

She'd always played by the rules, done what she was supposed to, tried to be the best that she could be. That included being a survivor. So, she'd done what the therapist had suggested—gone to the gravesite, read the police report, the coroner's report, the reports from the doctor who'd pronounced Kevin dead. She'd tried to heal, because that was what everyone had expected, and it was what she wanted to do.

Eight years later, she didn't know if she could heal from what she'd been through. The wounds had scarred over, but they weren't gone. They still throbbed and pulsed and ached every time something reminded her of Kevin.

Kevin, who apparently had a doppelgänger, one who knew who Virginia was and knew that Kevin had called her Ginny.

She shuddered.

Somewhere in the distance, a dog was barking. Officer Forrester's K-9 partner?

Maybe, and maybe they'd found the guy who'd been in the house. She knew enough about the Capitol K-9 Unit to know that every member was handpicked to do the job. They were all well trained, driven, hardworking. She'd seen that firsthand when one of the foster children she and Cassie were caring for had been in danger. The Capitol K-9 team had stepped in, protecting Cassie, Virginia and the kids.

Virginia had been more than happy to let them do it; but, then, she'd spent most of the past few years letting other people call the shots. It was so much easier to do that than to risk making a mistake, doing something that would get her into the kind of trouble she'd found herself in with Kevin.

She needed to change that. She knew it. She'd known it for a long time. Accepting the inheritance from Laurel was part of that. Taking control of her life, being less afraid and more courageous—that was the other part.

Sirens were screaming, and she knew the police were close. She could keep standing where she was or she could head back to the house and wait for them to arrive. A few weeks ago, she would have stayed put, but she had plans. Big ones. She wanted to open her own foster home, take the money she'd inherited and put it to good use. She really felt as if that was what God wanted her to do, but there was no way she could until she started taking control again, started regaining what she'd lost eight years ago.

She took a deep breath, ignoring the sick feeling of dread in the pit of her stomach as she headed back across the yard.

She bypassed the house, keeping a good distance between herself and the building. She didn't think the Kevin look-alike was still there. She'd heard Officer Forrester's dog howling, and she knew enough about K-9 work to know that meant he was on a scent.

She hated the house, though, and now she had new bad memories to add to the old ones.

A police cruiser was pulling into the driveway as she ran into the front yard. She waited, her heart pounding painfully as the officer climbed out. Midfifties with salt-and-pepper hair and a handlebar mustache that seemed out of place in Washington, DC, he had the rugged kind of hardness she'd noticed in the faces of a lot of veteran police officers.

"Ma'am?" he said. "Did you call about an intruder?"

"Yes." She moved toward him, her legs just a little shaky. She needed to get herself under control. The last thing she wanted was a full-blown panic attack. "He was in the house when I arrived."

"Is he still there?"

"I don't think so."

He nodded, called something in on his radio and turned toward the house, eyeing the closed front door and the empty porch. "I'll check things out."

"There was another officer here. He—"

"Yeah. We've got someone meeting him over at the bus depot. Wait here." He hurried into the house, and she was left standing in the yard.

She thought about calling Cassie and asking her to come. She didn't want to face things alone, but Cassie had enough on her plate. She didn't need to come running to the rescue every time Virginia had a little trouble.

Or a lot of it.

A second police cruiser pulled up behind the first. The passenger door opened, and Officer Forrester got out. He offered a quick wave before opening the back door and letting his dog out.

They made a striking team—both of them muscular and fit and a little ferocious looking. She'd met Officer Forrester at Cassie and Gavin's wedding. She hadn't paid all that much attention to him. She'd been trying to corral the kids, keep them from eating the cake or destroying flower arrangements. She'd heard a few of Cassie's other bridesmaids oohing and ahhing over the K-9 team members, but Virginia had no desire to ooh and ahh. She was way past the point of noticing men, and there was no way she planned to ever be involved in a relationship again.

"You doing okay?" Officer Forrester asked as he approached.

She nodded, because her throat still felt tight with fear, and she was afraid her voice would be shaky.

"I followed your guy to the bus depot. Samson lost the trail there. I think the perp might have gotten in a car, but it's possible he made it onto a bus. We'll check the security cameras in the area. See if we can figure out who he is and where he went."

"Good," she managed to say, her voice stronger than she expected it to be.

"You want to sit in your car while you wait?" he suggested, his gaze focused and intent, his eyes a bright crisp blue that reminded her of the summer sky.

"I'm fine."

"I'm sure you are, but you look pale, and Gavin asked me to keep an eye on you until he and Cassie get here."

"You called Gavin?"

"He's my supervisor," he responded as if that explained everything.

"Well, call him again," she said, because she didn't want her boss to come all the way from All Our Kids to help her. Not when there were two—she glanced at a tall blonde female officer getting out of the second cruiser—three police officers nearby. "Tell him that I'm fine and I don't need Cassie to come."

"How about you do that, Virginia?" he suggested. "I'm going in the house."

He was gone before she could respond, striding across the yard, Samson beside him.

She would have followed, but the female officer approached and began asking dozens of questions. Virginia answered the best she could, but her mind was on the house, the man she'd seen, the name he'd called her—Ginny. As if he'd said it a thousand times before.

No one called her Ginny. Not since Kevin had died.

No one in her new life, none of the new friends she'd
made, the people she worked with, the kids she took care
of knew that she'd ever gone by Ginny. For eight years,
she'd been Virginia.

Whoever the guy in the house had been, he'd known
her before. Or he'd known Kevin. She didn't like either
thought. She didn't want to revisit the past. She didn't
want to relive the weeks and months and years before
she'd nearly died.

What she wanted to do was go back to her safe life
working at All Our Kids. She wanted to forget about her
inheritance, her past, all the nightmares that plagued her.

The front door of the house opened, and Officer Forrester appeared, the responding officer right behind him.
They looked grim and unhappy, and she braced herself
for bad news as she followed the female officer across
the yard and up the porch stairs.

Virginia looked terrified.

John couldn't say he blamed her. Finding someone in
a supposedly empty house would scare the bravest person. From what Gavin had told him, Virginia wasn't exactly that. As a matter of fact, Gavin had said Virginia
tended to panic very quickly. Which was why he and
Cassie were on their way to the house.

He wasn't going to call and tell them not to come, but
Virginia seemed to be holding it together pretty well. No
tears, no screams, no sobs. Just wide blue eyes, pale skin
and soft hair falling across her cheeks.

"Did you find anything?" she asked, directing her
question to the other officer.

Leonard Morris was a DC police officer. Well liked
and respected, he knew just about every law enforcement
officer in the district. "Nothing to write home about,

ma'am," Officer Morris responded. "I'm going to dust for prints, but I thought you could come in, see if there's anything missing."

She hesitated for a heartbeat too long, her gaze jumping to the still-open front door, her skin going a shade paler. "I... Is that really necessary?"

Morris frowned. "If there's something missing, only you'll know it. So, yeah, I guess it is."

"I... Don't you want to dust for prints and look for evidence before I go in and contaminate the scene?"

"I think," John said, cutting in, taking her arm and urging her to the door, "it's been contaminated. You were already in there, remember?"

"I'm scared," she responded. "Not senile."

"Anyone would be scared in these circumstances."

"Maybe I didn't state my position strongly enough," she muttered as they stepped into the house. "I'm terrified, completely frozen with fear and unable to deal with this. Plus, up until today, I hadn't stepped foot in the house in eight years. I have no idea what Laurel had."

"You know what she had before. Maybe that will help. And you seem to be dealing just fine," he said, because she was. He'd seen people panic. He'd seen them so frozen with fear they couldn't act. Virginia didn't seem as if she was any of those things.

"For now. Let's see what happens if Kevin jumps out of a closet," she responded with a shaky laugh.

"Kevin?" Officer Morris asked.

Virginia frowned. "My husband. He died eight years ago."

"I guess he's not going to be jumping out of any closets, then," the female officer said, her gaze focused on the opulent staircase, the oil paintings that lined the wall leading upstairs. They screamed *money*. The whole place did.

"No. I guess he wouldn't, Officer…?"

"Glenda Winters. You want to tell me why you're worried about your dead husband jumping out of closets?" she asked.

John had worked with her before. She was a good police officer with a knack for getting the perp, but she was straightforward and matter-of-fact to a fault, her sharp interview tactics often getting her in trouble with her supervisor.

"I'm not," Virginia replied, walking into a huge living room, her gaze drifting across furniture, paintings and a grand piano that sat in an alcove jutting off from the main room. "It's just that the man who was in the house looked a lot like Kevin."

"They say everyone has a twin," Officer Morris commented.

"He called me Ginny. Just like Kevin used to," Virginia said, and for the first time since she'd come screaming through the bushes, John could actually see her shutting down and freezing up.

"Did Kevin have a brother?" he asked, and she shook her head, her eyes a little glassy, her skin pale as paper.

"No."

"How about cousins? Uncles? Extended family?" Officer Winters asked. "Because I have a cousin who looks so much like me, people think we're twins."

"If he does, I never met any of them."

"This was Laurel Johnson's place, right?" Officer Morris walked through the living room and into a dining area that could have seated twenty people comfortably.

"Yes. I'm her granddaughter-in-law."

Morris nodded. "She left you the property. Interesting, huh?"

Something seemed to pass between them, some unspoken words that John really wanted to hear, because there was an undercurrent in the house, a strange vibe that Virginia had brought inside with her. He wanted to know what it was, why it was there, what it had to do with the guy she'd seen in the house.

"I guess it is." Virginia took one last look around the living room. "As far as I can tell, nothing is missing," she said, then hurried into the dining room, the kitchen, up the back stairs and onto the second floor. With every step she seemed to sink deeper into herself, her eyes hollow and haunted, her expression blank.

Officer Morris whispered something in her ear, and she shook her head.

"I'm fine," she murmured, opening the first door and stepping into a nearly empty room. A cradle sat in the center of it, a few blankets piled inside. Pink. Blue. Yellow. There was a dresser, too. White and intricately carved, the legs swirling lion claws. No mementos, though. Not a picture, stuffed animal or toy.

"Everything looks okay in here," Virginia said, and tried to back out of the room.

Only John was standing behind her, and she backed into him.

He grabbed her shoulders, trying to keep her from toppling over. He felt narrow bones and taut muscles before she jerked away, skirted past him.

"Sorry."

"No need to apologize," he said, but she was already running to the next door to drag it open and dart inside.

THREE

Laurel had kept the nursery just the way it had been the day Kevin died. Being in it brought back memories Virginia had shoved so far back in her mind, she hadn't even known they were there—all the dreams about children and a family and creating something wonderful together, all the long conversations late at night when she and Kevin had shared their visions of the future. Only every word Kevin uttered had been designed to manipulate her, to make her believe that she could have all the things she longed for, so that he could have what he'd wanted—complete control. She'd believed him because she'd wanted to. She'd been a fool, and it had nearly cost her her life.

She wanted out of the house so desperately, she would have run downstairs and out the door if three police officers and a dog weren't watching her every move.

The dog, she thought, was preferable to the people. He, at least, looked sweet, his dark eyes following her as she moved through Laurel's room.

This was the same, too. Same flowered wallpaper that Virginia had helped her hang, same curtains that they'd picked out together in some posh bohemian shop in the heart of DC. Same antique headboard, same oversize rolltop desk that had been handed down from one generation to the other since before the revolutionary war.

It had always been closed before, the dark mahogany cover pulled down over the writing area and the dozens of tiny drawers and secret hiding places that Laurel had once shown her.

It was open now, and Virginia walked to it, ignoring the officers who walked into the room behind her. At least one of them knew her story. She wasn't sure how she felt about that. She'd refused to speak with reporters after the attack. It had taken a while, but eventually they'd lost interest and the story she'd lived through, the horrible nightmare that so many people had wanted the details of, had faded from the spotlight.

Eight years later, there were very few people who remembered. Those who did, didn't associate Virginia's face with the Johnson family tragedy. She'd never been in the limelight anyway. Kevin had preferred to stand there himself.

The older officer knew. He'd whispered a couple words that he'd probably thought would be comforting—
It's okay. He can't hurt you anymore.

Only the words hadn't been comforting.

They'd just made her want to cry, because she was *that* woman. The one who'd met and married a monster. The one who'd almost been killed by the person who was supposed to love her more than he loved anyone else.

She yanked open one of the desk drawers, staring blindly at its contents.

Something nudged her leg, and she looked down; the huge German shepherd sat beside her, his tail thumping, his mouth in a facsimile of a smile.

She couldn't help herself. She smiled in return. "Are

you in a hurry, Samson?" she asked, and the dog cocked his head to the side, nudging her leg again.

Not a "hurry up" nudge, she didn't think. More of an "I'm here" nudge. Whatever it was, it made her feel a little more grounded, a little less in the past and a little more in the moment.

She rifled through the drawer. Laurel kept her spare keys there. House. Car. Attic. She took that one, because she was going to have to check up there. The entire space had been insulated and made into a walk-in storage area filled with centuries' worth of family heirlooms.

She opened another drawer. This one had stamps, envelopes, beautiful handmade pens.

It took ten minutes to go through every drawer, to open every secret compartment. She took out a beautiful mother's ring that Kevin had presented to Laurel years before he met Virginia. Laurel had worn it every day, and as far as Virginia knew, she'd never taken it off. Not when Kevin had been alive.

She set the ring on the desktop and took a strand of pearls from another secret compartment. The jewelry piled up. So did the old coins and the cash—nearly a thousand dollars' worth of that. Laurel had liked to have cash on hand. Just in case.

"That's a lot of money, right there," Officer Forrester said quietly. "I'd think if the guy were here to steal, he'd have left the desk empty."

"Maybe he didn't have time to go through it." She rolled the desktop down, leaving the jewelry and money right where it was. The words felt hollow, her heart beating a hard harsh rhythm. She wanted to believe the guy had been there looking for easy cash but the sick feeling of dread in her stomach was telling her otherwise.

"That's a possibility," Officer Winters said, her voice

sharp. "It's also possible he found other valuables and took off with them. You said you hadn't been here in a while. He could have left with thousands of dollars' worth of stolen property."

I don't really care if he did. I never wanted any of this. I still don't, she wanted to say, but she didn't, because there wasn't a person she knew who wouldn't have celebrated the windfall Virginia had received. The few friends she'd told had given her dozens of ideas for what she could do with the money, the house, the antiques. Most of the ideas involved quitting her job, going on trips to Europe and Asia, traveling the country, finding Mr. Right.

She hadn't told anyone but Cassie that she didn't want the inheritance. Even Cassie didn't know the entire reason why.

Or maybe she did.

She was her boss, after all. There'd been a background check when Virginia had applied for the job. If the information about Kevin had come up, Cassie had kept it to herself. She'd never questioned Virginia, never brought up the life Virginia had lived before taking the job at All Our Kids.

That was the way Virginia wanted it.

No reminders of the past. No questions about why and how she'd ended up married to a monster. No sympathetic looks and whispered comments. She didn't want to be that woman, that wife, that abused spouse.

She just wanted to be the person she'd been before she'd fallen for Kevin.

It had taken years to realize that wasn't possible. By that time, keeping quiet about what she'd been through had become a habit. One she had no intention of breaking.

She walked to an old oil painting that hung between

two bay windows and pulled it from the wall, revealing the built-in safe that Laurel had shown her a year after she'd moved into the house, a day after Kevin had shoved her for the first time.

Maybe Laurel had thought seeing all the beautiful jewels that would be hers one day would keep Virginia from going to the police.

It hadn't.

Love had.

She hadn't wanted Kevin to be arrested. She hadn't wanted to ruin his reputation and his career. She'd believed his tearful apology, and she'd believed to the depth of her soul that he would change. She'd been wrong, of course. Sometimes, she thought that she'd always known it. Even then. Even the first time.

She knew the lock combination by heart, and she opened the safe. It was stuffed full of all the wonderful things that Laurel had collected over the years. Her husband had been generous. He'd showered her with expensive gifts.

She pulled out a velvet bag and poured six beautiful sapphire rings into her palm. Seeing them made her want to puke, because they were the first things Laurel had pulled out the day she'd opened the safe and shown Virginia everything she would inherit one day.

She gagged, tossing the rings into the safe and running to the en suite bathroom. She heard someone call her name, but she wasn't in the mood for listening. She slammed the door, turned the lock, sat on the cold tile floor and dropped her head to her knees.

If she'd had one tear left for all the lies she'd been told and believed, if she'd had one bit of grief for what she'd longed for and lost, she'd have cried.

She didn't, so she just sat where she was, the soft mur-

mur of voices drifting through the door, while she prayed that she could do what she knew she had to—face the past and move on with her life. It was the only way she'd ever find the sweet spot, the lovely place where she was exactly where God wanted her to be, doing exactly what He wanted her doing.

No more floundering around waiting for other people to call the shots. No more watching as life passed by. She wanted to engage in the process of living again. She wanted to do more than be a housemother to kids. She wanted to mentor them. She wanted to be an example to them. She wanted to be able to tell her story without embarrassment or shame, and she wanted other people to benefit from it.

That was what she thought about late at night when she couldn't sleep and all she had were her prayers and the still, soft voice that told her she was wasting time being afraid, wasting her life worrying about making the wrong choices.

She needed to change that.

The problem was, she wasn't sure how.

Someone knocked on the door, and she pushed to her feet, her bones aching, her muscles tight. She felt a thousand years old, but she managed to walk to the door and open it.

Officer Forrester was there, Samson beside him. The other two officers were gone.

"I'm sorry," she said. "I just—"

"You don't have to explain." He took her elbow, leading her back into the room.

"I feel like I do, Officer—"

"John. I'm not on duty." He smiled, and his face softened, all the hard lines and angles easing into something pleasant and approachable.

"You chased down the guy who was in my house."

"Tried to, but only because I was in the right place at the right time."

"Or the wrong place at the wrong time."

He chuckled. "I guess that depends on how you look at it. I see it as a good thing. But, then, I love what I do, and I'm always happy to step in and help when I can."

"That's…unusual."

"You seem awfully young to be so jaded, Virginia."

"I'm not young."

"Sure you are." He opened Laurel's closet, whistling softly. "Wow. This lady had some clothes."

"She did." She moved in beside him, eyeing the contents of the walk-in closet. Dresses. Shoes. Belts. Handbags. "I guess if the guy didn't take a bunch of cash and jewelry, he probably didn't take any of her clothes."

"Do you think that was what he was here for?" he asked. "Money?"

"That's what the police think he was here for."

"I'm not asking about the police. I'm asking about you. Do you think he was here for money or valuables?"

It was a simple question.

At least in John's mind it was.

Virginia didn't seem able to answer it.

She stared at him, her face pale, her eyes deeply shadowed.

"Okay. You're not going to answer that," he said. "So, how about you tell me why it's been so many years since you've been in the house?"

She shook her head. "It's not important."

"If it weren't, you'd be willing to tell me about it."

"Maybe I should have said that it's important to me but has no bearing on what happened today."

"You can't know that."

"The police seem to think—"

"I think that I already said that I'm not interested in what the police are saying. You know this house, you knew your grandmother-in-law. You knew your husband, and every time you mention that the guy who was here looked like Kevin, I can almost see the wheels turning behind your eyes. You're thinking something. I'd like to know what it is."

"I'm thinking that I could have been wrong about what I saw. Maybe the guy didn't look as much like Kevin as I'd thought." She closed the closet door and walked to a fireplace that took up most of one wall. There were a few photos on the mantel. He hadn't looked closely, but he thought they must be of Virginia's family. She lifted one, smiling a little as she looked at the image of a young man and woman in wedding finery. Probably taken in the fifties, it was a little faded, the framed glass covered with a layer of dust. She swiped dust from the glass, set it back down, and John waited, because he thought there was more she wanted to say.

Finally, she turned to face him again. "My husband wasn't the easiest man to live with. I have a lot of bad memories. I really don't like talking about them."

That explained a lot, but it didn't explain who had been in her house or why he'd been there.

"I'm sorry. I know that's got to be tough to live with," he said.

"Some days, it's harder than others." She looked around the room, and he thought she might be fighting tears. She didn't cry, though, just cleared her throat, and smoothed her hair. "I know you're trying to help, and I appreciate it, but Officer Morris already knows everything there is to know. If he's worried that this is connected to…my past. He'll let me know."

That should have been enough to send John on his

way. After all, this wasn't his case. Morris and Winters were calling the shots. He was just a witness who happened to be a police officer, but he didn't want to leave. Not when Virginia still looked so shaken.

"Morris is a great police officer, and he'll handle things well, but I'm your neighbor. If something happens, I'm the closest thing to help you've got. Keep that in mind, okay?"

"I will." She hesitated, her fingers trailing over another photo. "The thing is, something did happen. I almost died eight years ago. Right outside the front door of this place. Not even the neighbors were able to help. That's why I haven't been back. That's why I don't like talking about it. That's why I don't want to believe the guy I saw today has anything to do with Kevin."

The words were stated without emotion, but he read a boatload of feelings in her face. Fear, sadness, anxiety. Shame. That was the big one, and he'd seen it one too many times—a woman who'd done nothing wrong, feeling shame for what she'd been through.

"Your husband?" he asked, and she nodded, lifting another photo from the mantel. She was in it, white flowers in her hair, wearing a simple white dress that fell to her feet.

"This is my wedding photo. I guess Laurel cut Kevin out of it. We were married in Maui. A beautiful beach wedding with five hundred guests."

"Wow."

"I know. It was excessive. We footed the bill. I would have preferred to use the money to finish my doctorate, but Kevin…" She shook her head. "It was a long time ago. It doesn't matter."

"It matters to you," he responded.

"It shouldn't." She replaced the picture she was still

holding. "I should check the other rooms, see if anything has been disturbed."

She walked into the hall, and he didn't stop her.

He wanted to take a closer look at the photos on the mantel. The one of Virginia didn't look as if it had been cut. He opened the back of the frame and carefully lifted the photo out.

It had been folded.

He smoothed it out, eyeing the smiling dark-haired man who stood to Virginia's right. Not touching her. Which seemed odd. It was a wedding photo, after all. The guy had a shot glass in one hand, a bottle of bourbon in the other. He looked drunk, his eyes heavy-lidded, his grin sloppy.

He replaced the photo and looked at the others. Nothing stood out to him. They were all of the 1950s couple—marriage, new house, baby dressed in blue.

Kevin's father? If so, there were no other pictures of him. No toddler pictures. No school photos. No wedding picture. That made John curious. There was a story there, and he had a feeling that it was somehow related to the man who'd been in the house.

It wasn't his case, and it wasn't any of his business, but he planned to mention it to Morris. See if he knew more about the Johnson family than Virginia did.

Or more than she was willing to reveal.

That was going to have to change. There was no way she could be allowed to keep her secrets. She'd have to open up, say everything she knew, everything she suspected, because John had a bad feeling that the guy who'd been in her house had been after a lot more than a few bucks. He'd been after Virginia, and if she wasn't careful, he just might get what he wanted.

FOUR

The police thought the intruder had entered through the kitchen. The lock hadn't been tampered with, but there were a couple of muddy footprints on the back deck and a pair of old size ten boots sitting under the swing.

They weren't Kevin's. He'd always worn Italian leather. Dress shoes shined to a high sheen paired with suits he spent a small fortune on. Even if he'd worn boots, Virginia didn't think they'd have been sitting out on the back deck years after his death.

They belonged to someone. So did the clothes she'd found in the closet in the bedroom she hadn't wanted to enter. The bedroom she and Kevin had shared. She'd gone in anyway, found faded jeans and threadbare T-shirts hanging in a closet that had once been filled with Kevin's clothes. Kevin had never worn jeans, had rarely worn T-shirts. No, the clothes had belonged to someone else. Officer Morris had taken them as evidence. Virginia wasn't sure what kind of evidence he could get from them. Hair? DNA? She hadn't asked. She'd been too busy trying not to panic.

Now she was alone, the officers gone, the house silent. She paced the living room, cold to the bone. She'd turned the heat on high, turned every light in the house on. She'd made tea and drunk two cups, but she couldn't get warm.

Someone had been in the house.

Someone who'd looked like Kevin, who'd called her Ginny, who'd mocked her with words that had made her blood run like ice through her veins.

A friend of Kevin's?

If so, he wasn't someone she'd ever met.

Whoever he was, he'd been in the house for a while. The clothes, the boots. The police had agreed that the guy had spent some time there.

That meant he'd had plenty of time to take whatever he might have wanted, but the house seemed untouched, hundreds of valuable things left behind.

She rubbed her arms, trying to chase away the chill. It didn't work. It was the house, the memories. She'd thought about going to a hotel, but she had to do this, and she had to do it alone. Cassie had offered to stay the night, babysit her like she babysat the children at All Our Kids. Virginia had refused her offer.

At the time, the sun had still been up.

Now it had set, the last rays tingeing the sky with gold and pink. If she just looked at that, stared out the window and watched the sky go black, she might be okay.

She would be okay.

Because there was nothing to be afraid of. Gavin had changed the lock on the back and front doors; he'd checked the locks on all the windows. The house was secure. That should have made her feel better. It didn't.

She grabbed her overnight bag and walked up the stairs, the wood creaking beneath her feet. She knew the sounds the treads made. She knew the groan of the landing, the soft hiss of the furnace. She knew the house with all its quirks, but she still felt exposed and afraid, nervous in a way she hadn't been in years.

She thought about calling Cassie, just to hear some-one else's voice, but if she did that, Cassie would come running to the rescue.

That wasn't what Virginia wanted.

What she wanted was peace. The hard-won kind that came from conquering the beasts that had been control-ling her for too long.

Outside, the neighborhood quieted as people settled in for an evening at home. That was the kind of place this was—weekend parties and weeknight quiet. Older, well-established families doing what they'd done for generations—living well and nicely.

Only things weren't always nice there.

She'd learned that the hard way.

She grabbed a blanket from the linen closet. There was no way she was sleeping in any of the bedrooms. She'd sleep on the couch with her cell phone clutched in her hand. Just in case.

She *would* sleep, though.

She'd promised herself that.

She wouldn't spend the night pacing and jumping at shadows.

Only it had been years since she'd lived alone, years since she'd not had noise to fill the silences. The sounds of children whispering and giggling, the soft pad of feet on the floor, those were part of her life. Without them all she could hear were her own thoughts.

She settled onto the couch, pulling the blanket around her shoulders. It smelled of dust and loneliness. She tried not to think about Laurel, spending the last years of her life alone. No kids to visit her. No husband. No grand-children. Just Laurel living in this mausoleum of a house, shuffling from room to room, dusting and cleaning com-pulsively the way she had when Virginia lived there.

She couldn't sleep with that thought or with the musty blanket wrapped around her shoulders. She shoved it off, lay on her side, staring out the front window, wishing the night away.

She must have drifted off.

She woke to the sound of rain tapping against the roof and the subtle scent of cigarette smoke drifting in the air.

Cigarette smoke?

Her pulse jumped, and she inhaled deeply, catching the scent again. Just a tinge of something acrid and a little sharp lingering.

Was it coming from outside?

In the house?

She crept to the doorway that led into the hall and peered into the foyer. The front door was closed. Just the way she'd left it, but the scent of smoke was thicker there, and she glanced up the stairs, terrified that she'd see *him* again.

She saw nothing. Not him. Not the light that should have been shining from the landing.

The upstairs hallway was dark as pitch, and she was sure she saw something moving in the blackness. The shadow of a man? The swirl of smoke?

She didn't care. She wanted out.

She lunged for the door, scrambling with the lock and racing onto the porch. Her car was in the driveway, but she hadn't brought her keys, and the phone that she'd been clutching to her chest when she fell asleep? Gone.

She must have dropped it.

She should have thought to look for it before she went searching the house for a cigarette-smoking intruder.

She ran down the porch stairs, her bare feet slapping against wet wood. She made it halfway across the yard before she saw the man standing on the sidewalk. She skidded to a stop, her heart beating frantically, as she watched the butt of his cigarette arch through the darkness.

"Everything okay?" he asked, his face illuminated by the streetlights, his little dog sniffing around at his feet.

"I…" What could she say? That she'd smelled his cigarette and thought someone was in the house? She doubted he'd want to know all the details of that. "Fine…"

"Probably you should put some shoes on. This isn't just rain. It's ice—and your feet are going to freeze."

Her feet were already freezing, but she didn't mention that. She was too relieved to have found the smoker outside her house to be worried about her feet. She thanked him and walked back to the house. The door was open as she approached, just the way she'd left it.

She'd nearly reached it when it swung closed.

She grabbed the door handle, trying to push it open again.

It was locked.

She hadn't paid much attention when Gavin had been installing it. Was it the kind of knob that locked automatically?

One way or another, she was locked outside.

Which, she thought, might be for the best.

The door might have closed on its own. There was a slight breeze. It was also possible she'd imagined the shadow in the upstairs hallway. She'd imagined plenty of other things before—faces staring out of the dark corners of rooms she knew were empty, shadowy figures standing at the foot of her bed when she was just waking from nightmares. None of those things had ever turned out to be real, but right at that moment, she was certain someone was in the house, and she was just as certain that if she entered it, she might not come out alive.

She didn't have her phone, didn't know any of the neighbors. She'd given Gavin and Cassie the spare keys to the house, but she had no way of contacting either of them. She did know John Forrester, though, and he'd told her to call if she had any trouble. She didn't know what time it was. She didn't care. She jogged around the side of the house and headed toward his garage apartment.

Samson growled, the sound a soft warning that pulled John from sleep. He sat up, scanning the dark room for signs of trouble. The living room was empty, the TV still on whatever station John had been watching when he'd fallen asleep on the couch.

"What is it, boy?" he asked, keeping the light off as he walked to the window where the dog was standing.

The dog growled again, nudging at the glass, his gaze fixed on some point beyond the yard.

Virginia's house?

John leaned closer, peering out into the blackness. Ice fell from the inky sky, glittering on the trees and grass, tapping against the garage roof. Not a good night to be out, but he thought he saw a shadow moving near the shrubs. As he watched, it darted through the thick foliage, sprinted into the open.

Medium height. Slim.

Virginia?

Samson stopped growling, gave a soft whine that meant he recognized the person running toward the garage.

Virginia, for sure, and it looked as if she was in trouble.

He ran to the door, yanked it open. He was halfway down the stairs when Virginia appeared. She barreled toward him, wet hair hanging in her face, head down as she focused on keeping her footing on the slippery stairs.

"Everything okay?" he asked.

It was obvious everything wasn't.

She had bare feet, no coat, skin so pale it nearly glowed in the darkness.

"I'm running through an ice storm in bare feet," she responded. "Things are not okay."

"What's going on?" he asked, grabbing her hand, urging her up the last few stairs and into the apartment.

"I locked myself out of the house." Her teeth chattered, and he grabbed the throw from the back of the couch and dropped it around her shoulders.

"Should I ask why you were outside in the middle of the night?"

"I smelled cigarette smoke and thought it was coming from inside the house."

He didn't like the sound of that.

The police hadn't found cigarette butts on the property, but that didn't mean the guy who'd been there wasn't a smoker. "I'll go check things out," he said, grabbing Samson's work lead and calling the dog.

"Don't go rushing over there yet, John. I'm not done with my story."

"The ending isn't as exciting as the beginning?" he asked, grabbing a towel from the linen closet and handing it to her.

"I'm not sure." She wiped moisture from her face and hair, then tucked a few strands of hair behind her ear. "The cigarette smoke was coming from outside. Some guy walking his dog. When I went to go back in, the door closed."

"The wind?" he suggested, and she shrugged.

"That would be a logical explanation."

"But?" he prodded, because he thought there was

more to the story, and he wasn't sure why she was holding back.

"I'm going to be honest with you," she said with a sigh. "I was diagnosed with PTSD a few years ago. I went to counseling, worked through a lot of issues, but I still have nightmares. I still wake up in the middle of the night and think someone is standing in my room or hiding in the shadows. Sometimes I think there's danger when there isn't."

This was part of what she hadn't told him earlier. She'd hinted at it, said she'd nearly died, but she hadn't given details. He'd done a little digging and asked a few questions. Morris hadn't been eager to give details, but there'd been a few newspaper articles written about it. Local Attorney Shoots Wife and Self in Apparent Murder-Suicide Attempt.

Lots of speculation as to why it had happened, but there'd been no interviews with Virginia or her grandmother-in-law, so no one knew for sure how a seemingly rational high-level attorney could snap.

Personally, John didn't think he'd snapped. He thought the guy had been out of control from the get-go, that he'd just been hiding it from the world.

"The worst mistake you can make—" he began, taking the towel from her hand and using it to wipe moisture from the back of her hair. The strands were long and thick and curling from the rain, and he could see hints of gold and red mixed with light brown "—is hesitating to ask for help because you doubt your ability to distinguish real danger from imagined danger."

"I think I've proven—"

"You've proven that you're strong and smart," he said, cutting her off, because thinking about what she'd been through, the way she'd probably spent her entire marriage—in fear and self-doubt and even guilt—made him want to go back in time, meet her jerk of a husband and teach him a lesson about how women should be treated. "You might jump at shadows, but you're not calling for the cavalry every time it happens."

"I guess that's true," she conceded with a half smile. She had a little color in her cheeks, a little less hollowness in her eyes.

"So, tell me what happened with the door. You don't think it was the wind." Not a question, but she shook her head.

"I turned all the lights on in the house."

He'd noticed that, but he didn't say as much, just let her continue speaking.

"Then I went downstairs, lay down on the couch and fell asleep. When I woke, the lights upstairs were off."

"Power outage, maybe?"

"The other lights were still on."

"Did you check the circuit breaker? Maybe you blew a fuse. It happens in old houses."

"I might have checked, if I'd been able to get back in the house. The door locked when it closed. I couldn't remember if Gavin installed a lock that does that, but..." She shuddered and pulled the blanket a little tighter around her shoulders.

"I don't think he did." And that worried John. There'd been evidence that the guy who'd been in Virginia's house had stayed there for a while—clothes in the closet, an unmade bed. It could be that he'd returned, found a way in, gone back to whatever he was doing before Virginia had arrived. "Tell you what. Stay here. Samson and I will go check things out."

"I gave the spare key to Gavin and Cassie, and the doors are all locked."

"I'll call Gavin and ask him to meet me at your place.

I'll call Officer Morris, too. He should know what's going on." He attached Samson's lead, and every muscle in the dog's body tensed with excitement.

Samson loved his job, and John loved working with him. He was one of the smartest, most eager animals John had ever trained.

"Heel," he commanded as he stepped outside. "Lock the door, Virginia. I'll be back as soon as I can."

FIVE

John called Gavin on the way down the stairs and asked him to call Officer Morris. He didn't want to make the call himself. He knew what the DC officer would say—stay clear of the scene. Let the local police handle things.

Wasn't going to happen.

If someone was in the house, John planned to find him. Virginia had been through enough. He wasn't going to stand by and watch her be tormented. So far, that was what seemed to be happening. No overt threats of danger, no physical attacks, the guy seemed more interested in terrifying her than in hurting her.

That could change, though, and John wasn't willing to wait for it to happen.

The upstairs lights were on when John arrived at the house. He could see them gleaming through the windows. That didn't mean they hadn't been off when Virginia woke. He kept that in mind as he eased around the building, Samson sniffing the air, his ears alert, his tail high. Focused, but not cautious. So far, the dog didn't sense any danger.

They moved around to the front of the house, and Samson headed straight across the yard, sniffing at a soggy cigarette butt that lay on the sidewalk. It seemed odd that Virginia had been able to smell the smoke.

He left the butt where it was and walked to the porch, Samson on-heel. The dog nosed the floorboards, sniffed the air, growled.

"Find," John commanded, and the dog raced off the porch and around the side of the house, sniffing the ground, then the air. He nosed a bush that butted up against the edge of the house, alerting there before he ran to a window that was cracked open. No way had Virginia left it that way. Someone who'd been through what she had didn't leave windows open and doors unlocked.

Samson scratched at the window, barking twice. He smelled his quarry, and he wanted to get into the house and follow the scent to the prize.

"Hold," John said, and the dog subsided, sitting on his haunches, his eyes still trained on the window.

John eased it open. The screen had been cut, and that made his blood run cold. Virginia's instincts had been spot-on. Someone had been in the house with her.

A loud bang broke the silence, and Samson jumped up, barking frantically, pulling at the lead. John let him have his lead following him to the back of the house. A dark shadow sprinted across the yard. Tall. Thin. Fair skin.

"Freeze!" he called, but the guy kept going.

"Stop or I'll release my dog," he shouted the warning, and the guy hesitated, turning a little in their direction, something flashing in his hand.

A gun!

John dove for cover, landing on his stomach as the first bullet slammed into the upper story of the house. He pulled his weapon, but the perp had already darted behind the neighbor's house. No way was John taking a blind shot. It was too dangerous for the neighbors, for anyone who happened to wander outside to see what all the commotion was about.

He unhooked Samson's lead, releasing the dog, allowing him to do what he did best.

Samson moved across the yard, his muscular body eating up the ground. No hesitation. No slowing down. He had unerring accuracy when it came to finding suspects, and the guy they were seeking was close. No amount of running would get him out of range, because Samson would never give up the hunt.

John sprinted across the yard, knowing Samson would alert when he had the perp cornered. Ice crackled under his feet as he rounded the neighbor's house, racing into the front yard. Samson was just ahead, bounding across the street and into a small park lined with trees. The perp had plenty of cover there, plenty of places to hide and take aim.

"Release," he called, and Samson slowed, stopped, sending John a look that said *why are you ending the game?*

"Let's be careful, pal," John said, hooking the lead back on. "The guy has a gun." And he'd already discharged it.

They moved through the trees and farther into the park, Samson's muscles taut as he searched for the scent. When he found it, he barked once and took off running. The darkness pressed in on all sides. No light from the street here. Just the ice falling from the sky and the muted sound of cars driving through the neighborhood.

Behind them, branches snapped and feet pounded on the ground. A dog barked, and John knew that backup had arrived. He glanced over his shoulder, saw Dylan Ralsey and his dog Tico heading toward him.

"Gavin called. I was closer than he was, and he thought

you could use some backup," Dylan said as he scanned the darkness. "His ETA is ten minutes."

"Thanks," John replied. He didn't stop. They didn't have time to discuss what had happened, go over the details, come up with a plan.

"Tico was bored anyway. It's been a slow night." Dylan moved in beside him, flanking his right, Tico on his lead a little ahead.

The park opened out into another quiet street. Both dogs stopped at the curb, nosed the ground, whined.

"He had a car," John said, disgusted with himself for letting the guy escape.

"Wonder if any of the neighbors have security cameras? Seems like that kind of neighborhood, don't you think?" Dylan asked.

It did.

The houses were large, well maintained and expensive. Lights shone from porches and highlighted security signs posted in several yards.

"That would almost be too easy, wouldn't it? Look at some security footage, get a license plate number, find our guy?" he murmured more to himself than to Dylan.

"We can't assume the guy was driving his own car, but if we could get a tag number on whatever he was driving?" Dylan smiled through the darkness. "We'll have something to go on."

"Did Gavin mention whether or not Morris sent the clothes we found this afternoon to the evidence lab?"

"Not to me, but if they were sent, it might be weeks before you hear anything. If they can find some DNA, there might be a match in the system."

"Finding one will take even more time that Virginia might not have. The perp is bold. He entered the house while she was sleeping, and he had a gun."

"Did he fire it?"

"Hit the side of the house. The bullet should be lodged in the siding."

"We might get some ballistic evidence from it."

"You mean Morris might," John said. "He's the local PD who's handling the case."

"I know who he is. Gavin told me to steer clear of the guy."

"Guess Morris isn't all that happy with my involvement."

"From what Gavin said, he's on his way, and he's not happy. Said you needed to stop stepping on his toes or things could get ugly."

"Should I sit back and watch a woman be terrorized?" John asked, allowing Samson to nose the ground, follow whatever scent he could to the east.

"As a fellow member of the Capitol K-9 Unit, I'm going to have to say yes. Because that's the official protocol."

"What would you say as my friend?"

"You know what I'd say, John. Do what you have to do to keep Virginia safe."

"I guess you know which way I'm going to go," John responded, because he couldn't sit back and watch crimes be committed, he couldn't back off and wait for help to arrive when he could be the one doing the helping. It was the way he'd been raised. His father, grandfather, brother, had all been police officers. They'd all given their lives for their jobs, sacrificing everything to see justice done.

"I guess I do."

Samson stopped at a crossroad, circled twice, then sat on his haunches. He'd lost the trail. Not surprising. He was trained in apprehension and guard duty. Scent trail wasn't his forte, though he'd done some training in that, as well.

"Good try, champ," John said, scratching the dog behind the ears and offering the praise he deserved.

"The perp is heading toward downtown," Dylan said, his gaze focused on the road that led out of the community. "If we had a description of the vehicle, I could call it in, get some officers looking for it."

"Anyone who confronts the guy is going to have to be careful. He isn't afraid to use his weapon."

Dylan scowled. "That's not news that fills me with warm fuzzy feelings."

"I wasn't too thrilled, either."

"You'd be even less thrilled if you were lying in a hospital bed."

"True, but I don't think the guy was aiming for me. I think he was just trying to get me to back off."

"So, he's playing games?"

That was the feeling John had, so he nodded. "That's the impression that I'm getting."

He'd dealt with plenty of criminals. He'd had a few occasions when he'd been certain he was looking evil in the face. He was trained to understand the way felons would respond in a variety of situations, and he had a reputation for being good at staying a step ahead of the bad guys.

Sometimes, though, crimes weren't about what could be gained. They weren't about revenge or jealousy or passion. Sometimes they were a fantasy being played out, a game whose rules only the perpetrator knew.

He thought this was one of those times.

If he was right, the perp's next move couldn't be predicted. How he'd act or react couldn't be ascertained.

The best thing they could do was find him quickly

and get him off the street; because until he was locked away, Virginia wouldn't be safe.

One. Two. Three. Four. Five.

Virginia mentally counted houses with Christmas lights while she waited for Officer Morris to finish typing whatever it was he was typing into his tablet.

Six. Seven. Eight.

She hadn't learned much about what had happened at Laurel's place, but she could say for sure that John had a good view of the neighborhood from his kitchen window—houses, streets, the city beyond, all of it covered with a layer of ice that sparkled with reflected light.

It would be a mess for the commute in the morning, but right then, it was lovely. So were the Christmas lights hung from eaves and wound around columns and pillars. Several trees were decorated for the holiday. Most of them with soft blue or white lights. Very elegant and lovely, but that was the type of community they were in.

Nine. Ten. Eleven.

Officer Morris continued to type, and Virginia continued to count, because it was easier to do that than think about the gunshot she'd heard. No one had been injured. That's what Officer Morris had told her, but she hadn't heard from John, and she was worried.

Because worrying was something she excelled at. Apparently so was counting.

Dealing with emergencies? Not so much.

She almost hadn't opened the door when Officer Morris knocked. She'd been too afraid of who might be on the other side.

"Okay," Officer Morris said. "The report is filled out. We're good to go. How about we walk you back to your place, take a look around? Aside from a cut screen and busted window lock, I didn't see anything that looked out of place, but it would be best for you to take a look before I leave."

Her place.

Right.

She kept thinking of it as Laurel's or Kevin's or the Johnsons', but it belonged to her, and she had to go home to it. At least for the next few days.

"I should probably wait for John to return."

"He'll meet us at the house. I need to speak with him." There was no question in Officer Morris's voice. He had a plan, and he expected that everyone was going to follow it.

She didn't mind that. She didn't mind *him*. He seemed like a good guy, a nice cop. The fact that he knew what had happened to her…that was a little awkward, but he wasn't treating her with kid gloves, and she appreciated that.

She still didn't want to go back to the house.

Not after *he'd* been in it again. The guy who looked like Kevin. She hadn't seen him, but she was certain that was who it had been. Two different intruders in less than twenty-four hours seemed like too much of a stretch.

Yeah. It had been him. He'd broken the lock, cut the screen, entered the house. All while she'd been sleeping.

She shuddered, pulling the blanket John had given her closer.

Officer Morris's expression softened, and he touched her shoulder. "It's going to be fine, Virginia. He's gone. I promise you that."

She wasn't sure who he was talking about. The guy who looked like Kevin? Kevin?

Either way, he meant well, the words soothing and kind.

"Right. I know." She plastered a smile on her face. One that felt brittle and hard.

"I've been doing a little research," he said. Maybe he was hoping to distract her from the panic that was building. "Laurel Johnson was involved in a lot of charitable organizations."

"Yes," she responded, her mouth so dry it was all she could manage.

"One of them was the state prison ministry. She used to go there twice a week."

"I didn't know that."

"I doubt anyone did. She spent some time with one of the prisoners, helped him get his college degree. Name was Luke Miller. Ever heard of him?"

"No."

"He was released two months ago."

She wasn't sure what he was saying, what he was trying to get at. She was still thinking about going back to the house, walking into the place that had brought every nightmare she'd ever lived through.

"You look a little shaky. How about some water before we head over?" he suggested.

She nodded, mute with fear.

He walked into the kitchen, found a cup and filled it. "It really is going to be okay," he said, holding out the cup.

She took a step forward, felt the earth shake, the entire world rumble. For a moment, she thought she'd lost it, that it had finally happened, panic making her completely lose touch with reality. She was on the floor, staring up at the ceiling, smoke billowing all around her.

Officer Morris shouted something, and she rolled to her side, saw him lying under the partially caved-in wall, ice falling on his dark hair.

"Get out of here!" he shouted.

She struggled to her knees, her feet, grabbed the wood that was pinning him.

"Go!" he said again, and she shook her head, tugged harder, praying that somehow her strength would be enough to free him.

SIX

Smoke billowed up into the sky, flames licking the side of the garage as John raced toward his apartment. He'd expected trouble, but he hadn't expected this. He should have. He should have been prepared for anything.

Too late now.

The building was in flames, the interior exposed on the lower and upper levels.

A bomb?

That was what it looked like.

If there were more, they'd all be killed, but he wasn't going to wait for the fire department to show, couldn't wait for the bomb squad to be called in. Virginia and Officer Morris had been in the apartment. If they still were, they were in trouble.

"Hold!" he commanded, and Samson stopped short, his soft whimpers following John as he raced up the stairs that had been left untouched by the explosion.

The front door was closed. No time for a key, he kicked it in, smoke billowing out as it opened.

"Be careful!" Dylan shouted as he raced up the stairs behind him. "This place could crumble any minute."

That was John's fear. Getting in and out as quickly as possible was his plan.

Only God knew if that would happen, and John had to trust that His plan was best, that He'd see him through this like He had so many other things.

He pulled his shirt up over his mouth and nose, then headed into what had once been his living room. Part of the ceiling and wall had caved in, icy rain the only thing keeping the fire from taking over. Smoke billowed up through the floor and in through the collapsed wall. In seconds, the place would be pitch-black.

He scanned the room.

Virginia stood in the kitchen, tugging at lumber that had fallen, her frantic cries for help barely carrying above the roaring of the fire below.

He moved toward her and saw Officer Morris as he reached her side. His legs pinned by a heavy beam, his eyes open and filled with fury, he gestured toward Virginia.

"Get her out of here!" Morris shouted.

"I think we can free you," he responded, refusing to give in to panic, to let himself imagine the floor giving way.

Dylan moved in beside him. "On three," he said. "One. Two."

"Three." And the beam was up, Morris rolling out from beneath it.

Morris managed to get to his feet, but stumbled to his knees.

"My legs are busted," he growled, pushing to his feet again. Black smoke made it nearly impossible to see the extent of the damage, but there was no pain in his voice. No concern.

He was in shock.

Had to be.

They'd deal with it when they got out.

"When I catch the guy who did this," Morris muttered, "I'm going to make sure he goes away for the rest of his life."

An idle threat if they didn't get out.

"I'll get him," Dylan said, nothing but a shadow in the darkness. "You get Virginia."

No more words after that. No air for it. Just a sense of where the door should be, the direction they had to go to survive.

John grabbed Virginia's hand, leading the way through the thickening smoke.

He felt dizzy...knew how close they all were to losing consciousness. If he was heading in the wrong direction, if he'd gotten disoriented, they'd die.

He felt the front door before he saw it, the cold air billowing in and carrying bits of freezing rain with it.

He gave Virginia a gentle shove out the door.

"Get down the stairs," he rasped. "Stay close to Samson."

Then he turned, heading back into the darkness.

Dylan was there somewhere, struggling to carry Morris out.

John could hear Virginia calling his name, but he didn't turn back.

All of them or none of them.

That was the way it was going to be.

She couldn't leave them.

Wouldn't.

Virginia stood in the threshold of the door, smoke choking off her words as she shouted for the three men. She had no light to flash into the darkness, but she could scream until she had no voice left.

Behind her, sirens screeched and a dog howled.

Samson?

She didn't have time to comfort him. The building seemed to shake on its foundation, the fire eating away at the support beams.

"Over here!" she screamed. "This way!"

She thought she heard a voice, thought she saw something dark moving through the smoke.

Please, God, she pleaded silently as she shouted again.

Then they were there, just in front of her.

She reached in, dragging someone out by his shirt.

A Capitol K-9 officer. Morris plastered to his side, barely moving. Dylan? She thought that was the officer's name, but she didn't have time to ask, didn't have time to care.

"Down the stairs!" he shouted.

"John—"

"Here." John appeared in the doorway. "Now go! This place is going down."

She ran, stumbled down the last few steps and fell to her knees on wet grass.

And then John had her by the arm, dragging her up again.

"Keep going!" he shouted.

She didn't have time to wonder why; they were racing across the grass, the other K-9 officer right beside them, Morris in a fireman's hold over his shoulder.

Behind them, something popped. She heard a whoosh, felt a hot wind blow against her back. She stumbled, but John's arm was around her, and she kept going.

Just ahead, a fire crew raced toward them, shouting words Virginia couldn't hear.

Someone pulled her from John, slapped an oxygen mask over her face. She wanted to say that she was fine, that they needed to take care of the men, but darkness

was closing in. Not the night, the smoke, the icy storm—
just the blackness. She felt it coming for her, and then
she felt nothing at all.

If there was one thing John hated, it was hospitals.

He'd watched his father breathe his last in one, said
goodbye to his grandfather in one, been called to one
after his brother was fatally shot.

Yeah. Hospitals weren't his thing.

He strode to a sink in the tiny triage room they'd rolled
him into, and scrubbed soot from his face and hands. The
doctor had already been in once, listened to his lungs,
ordered an X-ray. Everything had checked out. Now, he
was waiting for aftercare instructions.

Whatever they were.

He opened the door, nearly walking into his coworker
Chase Zachary.

"You breaking out of this joint?" Chase asked, his coat
opened to reveal his uniform and firearm. He didn't have
his K-9 partner with him, though.

"Yes."

"You think that's a good idea?"

"It's a better idea than sitting here for another hour.
Besides, I need to check on Samson. A DC officer trans-
ported him to headquarters."

"Tico is there, too. Vet took a look at both. They're
good as gold and eating plenty of good food."

"Have you spoken with Dylan?"

"Just left him. He's fine. Gavin is with him."

"He's not with Virginia?" That worried him, and he
was ready to run down the hall, find her and make sure
she was okay.

"The little mousy assistant housemother?"

"She's not mousy."

"No." Chase grinned. "I guess it's all in the eye of the beholder. Heard they dug a bullet out of her house. I also heard your house is gone."

"It is." Which was something he hadn't thought too much about. He'd called the Hendersons from the ambulance. They were in Florida for the winter and hadn't seemed overly concerned about their destroyed garage. They hadn't stored anything there, and they had enough insurance and money to cover the loss. They had been concerned about him, though, and had promised to contact their insurance adjuster immediately.

He had renter's insurance and not enough stuff to be all that sorry for the loss of it.

"If you need a place to stay, Erin and I would be happy to have you," Chase offered.

"My landlords said I could stay in their house until the garage is rebuilt. They have an in-law suite in the basement that they're willing to rent me. I'm thinking I may stay at Virginia's for a while, though." He hadn't spoken with her about it, but she needed protection. He had a couple of friends in private security who owed him. He could call one in to help him out.

"You're worried about the guy returning?"

"He blew up a garage, Chase. He's capable of anything."

"You don't know it was him."

"I suspect it."

"Until you prove it—"

"I'm going to proceed with extreme caution. That means making sure he doesn't get another chance to hurt Virginia."

"Morris got the brunt of this one," Chase said grimly. "A broken tibia in his leg. Two broken bones in his foot. He'll be off work for a while."

"Did you talk to him?"

"He's not happy. He wants this guy off the street. He has a name. Some guy the Johnson woman used to visit in prison."

"Virginia?"

"No. The lady who used to own the home. Laurel? Morris said she spent a lot of time doing prison ministry. Interestingly enough, none of her friends knew about it. She didn't participate with her church group's prison ministry. She went with another church."

"Who was she visiting?"

"Guy named Luke Miller. He was put away when he was eighteen. Spent fourteen years in prison on grand theft charges. Got out two months ago."

"Any connection between him and Laurel?"

"Aside from the fact that Laurel helped him get his education? I don't know. Morris was digging for information, but he was coming up empty. I got the feeling he's going to keep digging even though he'll be out on medical leave for a while."

"What room is he in?"

"349."

"How about Virginia?" he asked.

"She left half an hour ago. The DC police escorted her to the house. They want to walk her through. Make sure nothing is missing."

He didn't like the sound of that. When they finished, would they leave her there alone? He wanted to visit with Morris, see how he was doing, pick his brain a little if he was up to it, but his first priority was making sure that Virginia was safe.

"They did that before. Nothing was gone. This guy has another agenda."

"What?"

"When I figure that out, I'll let you know." He walked into the hall, took a couple of steps, then realized he had no transportation.

He turned; Chase leaned against the doorjamb, waiting.

"Need a ride?" he asked with a smirk.

"I need answers more, but I'll take the ride if you're offering."

"You know I am," Chase responded. "Come on. Let's get out of here."

SEVEN

Laurel's bedroom had been torn apart. Every piece of clothing pulled from every drawer, every pair of shoes tossed from the closet, the place looked as if a tornado had torn through it.

"Looks like he did a pretty good job in here," one of the officers who had escorted Virginia home said.

"I guess so," she said, because she thought that was what he expected, but she didn't feel like replying. She felt like going back to All Our Kids, taking a shower, climbing into bed and forgetting everything for a while.

Her throat hurt, her eyes stung, her body ached. Soot covered her clothes, layered her hair. She'd washed her face at the hospital, but she still thought she could taste soot on her lips.

The fire had almost killed four people.

The guy who'd been breaking into the house, the one who'd crept around while she'd slept, he'd commit murder if he had a chance.

The police had assured her they weren't going to give him that.

She didn't know how they were going to stop him.

He'd already been in the house three times.

It didn't seem as if the threat of being discovered was

keeping him away. Instead of backing off, he'd escalated things. A bomb was what the police were saying. The FBI had been called in and a team was combing through the rubble left when the garage collapsed.

If she looked out the bedroom window, she knew she'd see spotlights gleaming through the darkness, all of them trained on what was left of John's home.

She didn't look.

She didn't want to relive the moment when the house had shaken, the wall had collapsed. If John and the other officer hadn't arrived, she and Officer Morris wouldn't have made it out.

"We're going to have an evidence team go through the room, so don't touch anything," a female officer said, snapping pictures of the mess. "The other rooms weren't touched. I don't think he had time to do more than this. Why don't you go downstairs? Make yourself a cup of tea? Relax while we process everything?"

Because I almost died, she wanted to say. *Because I can't relax until I know that the men who saved me are okay.*

She retreated anyway, walking through the hall and past the room she'd spent two years sleeping in. There were no photos of Kevin displayed in the house. She'd noticed that right away. None of the wedding photos that had once hung from the walls. None of the family photos that Laurel had insisted they have taken every year. It was as if Laurel had tried to erase her grandson from the property. His clothes were still in the bedroom, but other than that, every trace of him was gone.

Funny how time could change memories. Now the things that Virginia had once loved about Kevin had become nothing more than red flags that she'd missed. The lavish gifts, the sweet words, the soft kisses, all of those had been part of the game Kevin had been playing. How far could he go? How much could he push? How deeply could he make Virginia love him?

How much could he hurt her before she ran away?

She guessed they had both figured that out.

She shuddered, the sound of voices drifting up the stairs as she approached the landing. She didn't want to face the people there. Police officers, FBI, fire marshals, members of the Capitol K-9 team, all of them were milling in and out of the house, trying to find answers she didn't think would be found.

She turned around, headed for the back of the house and the door that led up into the attic. It had been locked since she'd arrived, and she hadn't bothered to get the key from Laurel's room. She knew there was another in the vase that sat on a shelf in one of the wall niches that had been added to the house years ago. Before Laurel's time. That's what her grandmother-in-law had told Virginia when she'd given her a tour of the property. Virginia had been blown away by the opulence and grandeur. Everywhere she'd turned there'd been treasures to see. She liked to believe that she hadn't been swayed by all that marrying Kevin offered. She'd loved him deeply at that point, and she'd have been willing to live in a hovel if it had meant being his wife.

She swallowed down bitterness, the acrid scent of smoke swirling around her as she grabbed the vase, dumping the key into her palm. A folded photograph fell out with it.

She carried it with her as she unlocked the attic door and walked up the steps. She turned on a light in the cavernous room. It was quiet there, nothing but the sound of icy rain filling the silence.

Leather trunks still lined the walls, dozens of boxes

interspersed between them. She knew one had Christmas decorations and that another had all Kevin's baby clothes and toys. Several pieces of furniture sat in the center of the finished space—a leather chair that had belonged to Kevin's grandfather, a rocking chair that Laurel had rocked her only son in, the crib that they'd talked about carrying down to the nursery when Virginia and Kevin had children. Every item had a story, but none of the stories had happy endings.

Kevin's mother had given birth to him and then run off with another man. His father had died of a drug overdose a year later, leaving Laurel and her husband to raise their grandson. Now Kevin was gone. Laurel and her husband were gone. Nothing remained of their lives but boxes of things and a house filled with stuff that had never made any of them happy.

Virginia sat in the rocking chair, the key still clutched in one hand, the picture in the other. It hadn't been in the vase before she'd been shot. She knew that for sure. She'd gone into the attic many times during her marriage, creeping up the stairs in the middle of the night to sit in the darkness and pray that her marriage would be healed, that Kevin would be changed.

But God didn't force people to do the right thing, and Kevin's faith had been a facade, lip service to what he'd been raised to believe. There'd been no depth to it, no desire to grow closer to God or to anyone else. Kevin had loved himself. Above all and above everything, getting what he wanted was his primary motivation.

Her eyes burned, but she didn't cry.

It was too late for that, too late to change one thing that had happened.

Footsteps sounded on the attic stairs, but she didn't get up. She didn't have the energy or the motivation to go back downstairs, look through all the rooms that should have been filled with family and love but were filled only with treasures that couldn't fill the holes in her heart.

"Virginia?" John said quietly, stepping into the room, his clothes still covered with soot and ash.

"I'm here," she said, the words hot and dry and hard to speak. There was too much in her throat—too many emotions, too much loss.

"Listening to the sound of the rain on the roof?" he asked, taking a seat in the leather chair beside her. "Or escaping the chaos that is going on downstairs?"

"Neither," she responded. "Both."

He laughed softly, the sound mixing with the rain and the whistle of wind beneath the eaves. "They'll be gone soon."

"I wish I could be."

"You can be. Nothing is holding you here."

"You're wrong." She met his eyes and saw something in his gaze that made her pulse jump. Kindness, compassion, concern, those were things she hadn't ever had from Kevin. Maybe she was greedy for them. Maybe she was searching for something that had been missing from every relationship she'd ever been in. Her parents had been drug addicts, her grandparents had been bitter about having to raise their daughter's child. She'd been shuffled from one home to another for years, each family member a little less caring than the last.

She'd found her way, though. She'd gotten her degree, found a job she'd loved.

Fallen for a guy who could never love her.

She turned away from John, her heart beating frantically.

"You can do whatever you want to do, Virginia," John

said, taking the key from her hand, smoothing out the crescents she'd dug into her palm.

She hadn't felt the pain, but she felt the warm roughness of his fingers. Felt it all the way to her toes.

She tugged away, wiping her palm on her sooty jeans. Even then, she could feel the warmth of his touch.

"What I want is to live my life the same way everyone else does. Without all the baggage and all the memories. I've been trying to do that for years, but it hasn't happened," she muttered, her heart beating a little too fast, her cheeks just a little too warm. "So I'd say you're wrong. I can't do whatever I want. No one really can."

"I guess," he said, slipping the photo from her hand. "That depends on whether or not the person is brave enough to go after what he wants."

"What's that supposed to mean?"

"Just that it's easier to hide from ourselves than it is to hide from anyone else."

"I'm not in the mood for riddles," she murmured.

"No riddle. Just truth. Until you stop feeling guilty about what happened, you're not going to be able to move on."

"I don't feel guilty," she protested, but he was right. She did. If she'd just been smart, strong enough, confident enough none of this ever would have happened. She'd have walked away from Kevin the first time he'd criticized and demeaned her, she'd have left him before the first shove, the first slap, the first threat.

"Like I said, it's a lot easier to hide from ourselves than it is to hide from others." He unfolded the photo and smoothed it out. "What's this?"

"I don't know," she responded, eager to change the subject. Happy to do it. She didn't like that he saw her so clearly, didn't like that she could look in his eyes and see so many things that she'd spent her entire life longing for.

"Looks like a school picture. Kevin's maybe?" He handed it to her, and she studied the class photo. "Fifth grade" was scrolled across the bottom, "Mr. Morrow" and the school year written beneath it. A list of children's names was to the side. Left to right. Front to back.

Not Kevin's fifth-grade photo. Laurel had kept those in a photo album in her closet. Neatly dated, little stick-on arrows pointing to her grandson. Kevin had always been the only kid wearing a tie on picture day. He'd told her once that he'd hated that, told her that he'd hated being raised by people who were too old to understand times changed, cultures changed.

He hadn't had much respect for his grandparents.

He hadn't had much respect for anyone.

"This isn't Kevin's. He would have been in third grade the year it was taken."

"You're sure?"

"Positive. We were the same age, graduated high school the same year. Besides, all the students are listed. His name isn't there."

"You said Laurel didn't have any other grandchildren?"

"Kevin's dad was her only child. He died when he was twenty. A year after Kevin was born."

"He was a young father."

"He and Kevin's mother were pretty heavy into the drug scene. He overdosed. She went to jail, came out clean and went back on the streets a few years later. Lauren said she overdosed when Kevin was ten. He never knew his mother, so I guess it didn't impact him much."

"Where'd you find this?" he asked, taking the photo from her hand again, turning it over as if there might be something on the back that would reveal its secrets.

"In the vase where Laurel kept the spare attic key."

"That's an odd place for a picture."

"It wasn't there when I lived here. She put it there after…"

"It meant something to her, then. Otherwise, she'd have thrown it away. Did you come up here often?"

"A few times a week."

"And you used the key in the vase?"

"Yes."

"Did Laurel know that?"

"She's the one who showed me where it was."

"Then maybe she was trying to show you something else with this. Tell you what—" He stood, offering his hand. "Let's go get Samson. He's at K-9 headquarters. We can use the computers there. See what we can dig up about these kids."

She could have refused, but she was tired of sitting in the old house, listening to her own thoughts. She was tired of feeling trapped by her fears and by the man who seemed determined to make her relive her nightmares.

She took John's hand, allowing herself to be pulled up.

He didn't release his hold as they descended the stairs, and she didn't pull away. She didn't ask herself what that meant. She didn't want to know. She just wanted to find the guy who was terrorizing her, sell Laurel's house and move on with her life.

EIGHT

"No," Virginia said as John pulled into the parking lot at Capitol K-9 headquarters.

He'd outlined his plan for keeping her safe.

She hadn't liked it.

He didn't think many people would like the idea of having strangers living with them twenty-four hours a day, seven days a week.

"The perp isn't playing with a full deck, and he's not playing by any rules any of us can follow."

"I know," she responded, her voice tight, her entire body tight. Muscles taut, expression guarded, she looked ready for a fight.

He didn't plan to give her one. That wasn't the way he operated. Years of helping his mother raise his siblings after their dad passed away had taught him everything he needed to know about winning arguments. Teenagers were tough. Compared to his three younger siblings, Virginia was going to be a piece of cake. She was older, smarter, wiser. And she knew her own mortality, wanted to live, wanted to move on, live life without all the baggage weighing her down.

He'd heard the longing in her voice when they were sitting in the attic. He'd wanted to promise her that everything would be okay, that she'd have what she so desperately wanted.

"If you know, then why are you refusing to let me help you?" he asked.

"Because helping me isn't your responsibility. The DC police are in charge of the case."

"That doesn't relieve me of my obligation to care for my neighbors and my friends," he responded, getting out of the SUV and rounding the vehicle. The storm had passed, but the sky was still gray with thick cloud cover, the blacktop glistening with ice.

Virginia was already out of the vehicle by the time he reached her door. She'd changed before they'd left the house, and the jeans and T-shirt she wore were free of soot, her coat clean. He could still smell smoke in her hair. Or maybe he was smelling it on his clothes and skin. He hadn't bothered trying to find clothes to change into. Everything he owned was in the apartment. He'd be surprised if any of it could be salvaged.

"I don't want to be anyone's obligation," Virginia said as he cupped her elbow and led her to the building.

"Obligation isn't a bad thing."

"It is if you're on the receiving end of it."

"There are a lot worse things to be on the receiving end of—guns, knives. Bombs. Just to name a few." He opened the door and ushered her into headquarters. Someone had put a tree up in the foyer, its boughs covered with ornaments.

"I get that. I just…don't want to owe anyone."

"That's a foolish reason to die, Virginia," he said, the words blunt and a little harsh. He meant them to sound that way, meant for her to understand just how important it was that she have twenty-four-hour protection.

She didn't say anything. Not as they took the elevator up to the third floor. Not as he led the way to his office. Not as she settled into a chair across from his desk.

"I'm going to get Samson. Wait here."

He made it to the door, stepping into the hall when she finally spoke.

"All right," she said quietly. "You and your friend can stay at the house. I'm going to pay you, though. Whatever the going rate is for private security."

That wasn't going to happen.

He didn't tell her that.

Just nodded and walked into the hall.

It didn't take long to retrieve Samson from the kennel. Headquarters was quiet this time of night, most team members either out on guard duty or running patrol. Samson barked happily as John opened the kennel, attached his leash and headed back to the office.

Virginia was standing at the window when he entered the room. She'd pulled her hair into some kind of twist, and he could see her nape, the soft tendrils of hair there and a thick white scar that curved from just behind her ear down into her shirt.

He knew he shouldn't, told himself not to, but he touched the scar, his finger tracing the jagged curves. "Did he do this to you?" he asked, and she turned, meeting his eyes.

"No." She smiled but there was no pleasure in it. "I did it to myself. I was six and determined to find my mother. I tried to climb from a second-story window into an old oak tree. It didn't work out."

"Where was your mom?"

"On the streets somewhere. She was clean for most of the first six years of my life. Then…" She shrugged. "She gave in to the cravings, and the drugs became way more important than I was."

"I'm sorry," he said, and she smiled again.

"I spent a lot of time being sorry, too, then I almost died and I realized that I hadn't done anything to make her leave and that I never could have been enough to make her stay. Once I understood that, it didn't hurt so much."

"You've had a rocky road, haven't you?" he asked, touching her cheek, letting his palm rest against her cool skin.

"Not as rocky as some people. How about you?" she asked as she bent to scratch Samson's head.

"My road has been pretty smooth," he responded. His father's death had been difficult, but his family had had support and love from friends, family and the community. Losing his brother had been devastating, but he'd had other siblings to think about, his mother to focus on. And he'd had his faith. It told him that goodbye wasn't forever, that he'd see his father, brother and grandfather again. That didn't make the loss easy, but it did make it bearable.

"Did you grow up in the suburbs with a mother and father and a couple of siblings? Did you eat meals together every night and go to church every Sunday?"

"Something like that. Until my father died. Then things got a little more difficult."

"I'm sorry, John. Was he ill?"

"He was a police officer. Killed in the line of duty. We lost my grandfather and brother the same way."

"Your road wasn't nearly as smooth as you made it out to be." She touched his wrist, and he captured her hand and tugged her a step closer, because there was something about her that made him want to look a little longer, see a little more of who she was.

"Every road has a few bumps," he said, because it

was true, and he didn't waste much time feeling bad because he'd hit a few. "Now, how about we take another look at the picture?"

The picture. Right.

Virginia had been so busy looking into John's eyes, she'd forgotten that they had a reason for being in his office. One that didn't include long conversations about their pasts, about their families, about the things they'd been through.

He sat behind the desk, and she took the seat across from him, pulling the photo out of her coat pocket and flattening it against the desk. "There must be someone Laurel knew here. She didn't keep things just to keep them."

"You're sure about that?" he asked. "Because from the look of the house, I'd say she liked to collect lots of things."

"She did, but everything she collected had value or meaning. She never kept something just to keep it." As a matter of fact, Laurel had had a story for every item in the house. Some of the stories had been passed down to her, some she'd lived. She might have joined the Johnson family through marriage, but she'd embraced the history of it with a zeal that Virginia was never able to match. "If she kept this, she did it because it was important to her."

"Important how?" he asked, and she studied the photo, scanning the names, the teacher, the first row of kids, the second row.

"I don't..." Her voice trailed off as she got to the end of the third row. A boy stood unsmiling just a little apart from the group. He had dark hair. Kevin had been blond when he was in grade school. It was the face that made her pause. The high cheekbones, the cleft chin, the eyes.

He looked so much like Kevin had at that age, they could have been brothers.

"What's wrong?" John leaned forward, his hand brushing Virginia's as he turned the photo so that he could see it more clearly.

"This," she responded, jabbing at the boy. "Could be Kevin. Except for the dark hair."

"What's his name?"

She ran her finger along the list of kids until she landed on the correct one. "Luke Miller."

The name tripped off her tongue, and her pulse jumped. "That's the name of the guy—"

"Laurel visited in prison," he finished, lifting the photo, eyeing the boy who'd turned into a man who'd spent more than a third of his life in jail.

"She also helped him get his college education," she said quietly.

"I wonder what else she did for him?" John murmured, turning on his computer, typing something in. He printed a page, then passed it over to her. "Look familiar?" he asked.

Her blood ran cold as she looked into the face of the man she'd seen on the stairs. Light brown hair. Hazel eyes. Prison orange.

A mug shot?

"This is the guy I saw," she confirmed, and John typed something else.

"According to our records, he's living in Suitland, Maryland, in a halfway house for recovering addicts. Last time he checked in with his parole officer was last week."

"Suitland isn't far," she said, and he shook his head.

"Twenty-minute drive without traffic. He could be leaving and returning without garnering too much attention. Or he could have walked out and not returned."

"Walked out and gone to Laurel's house, you mean? Squatted there because he knew she wasn't returning?"

"It's a good possibility." He took out his cell phone and texted someone. "I'm contacting Margaret Meyer. She runs Capitol K-9. If anyone can get several law enforcement entities working together, she can. Hopefully we can have this guy back behind bars in a few hours."

"From your lips to God's ears," she replied, walking back to the window that looked out over the parking lot.

They were in the middle of DC, and the lights from dozens of buildings glowed through the darkness. Wreaths hung from the streetlights. Red Christmas bows decorated a fence that surrounded the parking area. The holidays were approaching, and the world was preparing. All Virginia wanted to do was hide.

"It's going to be okay, Virginia," John said, his arm sliding around her waist. He didn't offer a million words to try to reassure her. He didn't tell her all the reasons why her fears were unfounded. He just stood beside her, the soft silence of the building, the warmth of his arm on her waist oddly reassuring.

"I'm not hanging my hat on that," she said quietly, and he chuckled.

"Ever the optimist, huh?"

"I prefer to be realistic."

"Realistic and hopeful. That's the best combination."

Hopeful? It had been a long time since she'd felt that, years since hope had bubbled up and spilled out into her life. She wasn't sure she remembered what it felt like. Sunrise, maybe? The first day of a new year? Christmas morning with presents under the tree? Life stretched out before her, a hundred possibilities there for the choosing?

Only she'd chosen Kevin. Her biggest and most lasting mistake. Her chest itched where the bullet had entered, the old wound healed over now, but still there. Every time she looked in the mirror, she was reminded of just how lousy her decision-making ability could be, and each time she was reminded, she vowed not to make the same mistake again.

"I'm not sure I remember what hope feels like," she admitted, the words spilling out. "I only remember what it's like to have it crushed."

"Disappointments are inevitable," he said, turning her so that they were facing each other, his gaze solemn, his hands soft as they cupped her shoulders. "Being destroyed by them is not."

"I haven't been destroyed," she responded, because she'd gone on, she'd made a good life for herself.

He studied her for a moment, his blue eyes as sharp and crisp as a fall morning.

"No. I guess you haven't. Just make sure you haven't been diminished by it, either. Come on. My friend is going to meet us at the house. He can run guard duty while you and I dig around, see if we can figure out what the connection is between Laurel and Luke."

"They must be related," she said as they walked into the corridor, Samson trotting beside them. "Laurel believed in family above almost anything else. If Luke was part of the family, she'd have done anything to help him."

"If that's true, there will be evidence of it. We just have to find it."

She would rather go back to All Our Kids. She'd rather forget all about the house, the Kevin look-alike, the secrets that Laurel had obviously been keeping.

She'd rather, but she doubted that would keep her safe, so she allowed herself to be led through the building and back out into the wintry night.

NINE

First days cooped up in the house with two men was starting to get to Virginia. Much as she wanted to enjoy her extra time off, she couldn't. The walls were closing in around her, the itemized lists of antiques and collectibles growing longer every day, because that's what she spent most of her time doing—going through every drawer, every closet, every cupboard and shelf, writing down Laurel's treasures.

She still hadn't found anything that would link Luke Miller to the Johnson family. The police hadn't been able to find a connection, either. Luke had grown up a few miles from the Johnson's posh neighborhood. His mother had been in and out of his life, and he'd been raised by his maternal grandmother in a community of low-income apartments. He'd been smart enough and driven enough to earn a scholarship to the prestigious school that Kevin had attended.

Maybe that's how Laurel had met him?

She wasn't sure and didn't have the freedom to leave the house and go searching for answers.

She was trapped like a rat.

For her own safety. That's what Gavin had said when he'd told her that she needed to stay put until Luke was apprehended. She'd planned to return to work at the beginning of the week. Instead, she was living in the one place she'd vowed to never return to.

"Irony," she said, and Samson lifted his head, cocking it to the side. John and another Capitol K-9 officer were having a meeting of the minds in the kitchen. Dylan seemed like a nice guy. That didn't mean she wanted to spend the better part of five days hanging around him.

Unfortunately, there hadn't been any leads. Luke had walked out of the halfway house and dropped off the grid.

Virginia hoped that he'd drop back on soon, because she wanted to get back to her life. She had Christmas cookies to bake with the kids, a house to decorate, a tree to put up. All the little traditions that she and Cassie had put into place when they'd begun working together needed to be revisited for the sake of the children who'd been with them long-term. Some of those kids had never had traditions, had never experienced constancy. They craved routine and familiarity like other kids craved ice cream or sweets.

Right now, they were missing Virginia desperately.

She heard it in their voices every time she called All Our Kids to check in—worry tinged with betrayal. She'd always been there for them. Now she wasn't.

That hurt them and it hurt her.

The sun had set hours ago, and she'd called just before the youngest of the foster kids' bedtime. She'd said goodnight to each child, heard various renditions of the same theme: *When are you coming home? Why do you have to be away for so long?*

How could she explain without worrying kids who already worried too much?

She'd made it simple. Just told them that cleaning out

85

the house was taking a long time. Eventually that excuse wasn't going to work. Eventually, she needed to return.

Eventually meaning sooner rather than later.

Too bad she didn't have any control over things.

She scowled, yanking open the bottom drawer of the dresser that sat against the wall in the blue room. Laurel had always called it that, and Virginia had never figured out why. It was the brightest room in the house. Not a speck of blue in any of the decorations. No dark wood furniture or paneling. The wallpaper soft yellow with tiny white roses sprinkled across it. White wainscoting covered the lower portion of the walls. Even the furniture was white—the canopy bed sitting in the middle of the wood floor.

"It's a little too much, if you ask me," she said, and Samson huffed, setting his head back down on his paws. He'd prefer to be with John, but he'd been commanded to stay with her. Something John did every time he had a meeting to attend or business that needed doing.

John…

He was turning into a problem.

No matter how much she tried not to like him, no matter how many times she told herself that he was just a guy helping her out, a guy who would disappear from her life as soon as Luke had been apprehended, she couldn't stop her pulse from leaping every time he entered the room, couldn't stop the warmth that settled in her heart every time she looked in his eyes.

He was…special.

Not in the phony, fake way Kevin had been. John was exactly what he seemed to be—strong, determined, caring.

He'd brought a box of Christmas decorations the previous day, telling her that it was time to make the place a little more festive. What he'd really been trying to do was get her mind off Luke, Kevin, Laurel—a dozen things she could do nothing about.

She'd wanted to ask him to take the decorations away, but she'd looked into his blue eyes, seen the compassion and concern there, and she'd found herself hanging a garland from the banister and bows from fireplace mantels.

"He's going to be a problem," she said as she lifted a stack of tablecloths from the drawer.

"Who?" John said, his voice so unexpected, she jumped.

"You," she responded honestly, jotting a note on her tablet—*Five lace tablecloths. Old. Handmade?*

"Should I be flattered or chastised?" he asked, settling onto the floor beside her, a soft smile easing the hard lines of his face.

"That depends."

"On?"

"Whether you like being a problem."

"That depends," he replied, taking the tablet from her hand and setting it on the dresser.

"On?"

"What kind of problem we're talking about." He stood and pulled her to her feet, his dark jeans and dark T-shirt brand-new. He hadn't shopped for them, had barely left the house the past few days. Coworkers had delivered the things he'd needed, bringing by several items that had been salvaged from the fire.

Mostly, John's belongings had been destroyed.

He'd never once complained. Just gone through the process of replacing them. Not an easy task when he spent every moment of his days babysitting Virginia.

She frowned, closing the drawer and walking to the lone painting that hung on the wall. It was the only decoration. Unlike every other room in the house, the blue room was devoid of knickknacks and collectibles. Aside from the one painting, nothing hung from the wall. Everything was simple and elegant, understated and pretty.

"You're the kind of problem—" she began as she lifted the painting from its hook. Beneath it was one of three wall safes that had been installed decades ago. She'd already been through the other two "—that could break a girl's heart if she let it."

There. She'd said it. What she'd been thinking for days. If she let herself, she could fall for John. If that happened, she'd end up hurt. It was inevitable, right? Because she had no ability to choose things that were good for her, men who would treat her well.

Hadn't she proven that?

"To break someone's heart," he said as she turned the combination lock. "I'd have to do something to hurt her."

"To break someone's heart," she responded as she opened the safe, "you'd simply have to walk away."

"Are we talking about you, Virginia?" He turned her so that they were face-to-face, and she couldn't help looking straight into his eyes. "Because once I commit to someone, I don't walk away."

"We're not committed. Not even close," she pointed out.

"But we could be. If we let ourselves head in that direction."

"I've made too many mistakes, and I—"

"Don't trust yourself enough to know you've learned from them?" he asked, his voice a little rough, his finger gentle as he traced a line along her jaw and down to the pulse point in her neck. His finger rested there, and she knew he could feel how quickly her heart was beating.

"Maybe. Or maybe I'm just afraid of being hurt. I'm afraid of finding out that something I've pinned my hopes on is just a facade, a trick of the light and of my mind."

She turned back to the safe, reaching blindly for a pile of papers, her eyes burning with tears that shouldn't have been there.

She'd cried herself out years ago, but a tear slipped down her cheek anyway, dropped onto the papers she was holding.

"Don't cry," John said softly, pulling her into his arms, his hands smoothing her hair, resting on her back. She should have stepped away. She knew she should have, but she burrowed in closer, let her head rest against his chest, let her arms slide around his waist.

This was where she wanted to be. Right here. With this man. It didn't matter that they were in a house she'd spent years hating. It didn't matter that she'd lived a dozen nightmares in the room down the hall, in the kitchen below, in the hallway and on the porch. It didn't matter, because John filled the dark places, made her feel strong when she'd only ever felt weak.

"It's going to be okay," he said. "I promise."

"Promises are a dime a dozen," she replied, and he chuckled.

"We really do need to work on your optimism." He stepped back, wiped the moisture from her cheeks. "Anything interesting in that safe?"

"Just papers." She glanced down at what she was holding—a birth certificate. The name scrawled across it made her pulse jump.

"It's his," she said, holding it out to John. "Luke Miller."

This was it.

Exactly what they needed to prove the connection between Luke and Laurel. Birth certificates didn't lie, and this one listed Ryan Johnson as Luke's father. His mother was a woman whose name John had never heard mentioned—Alice Randal. Both were dead. Not Kevin's mother.

".Ryan was your father-in-law?" he asked, and Virginia nodded.

"He must have had another son a few years before Kevin was born."

"Laurel never mentioned it." She frowned, tucking a few strands of hair behind her ear. "Neither did Kevin."

"They knew. Or Laurel did. Looks like she was paying good money for the woman to keep quiet." John set the birth certificate on the dresser and took the stack of papers from Virginia's hands. Paternity test results, stacks of cashed checks written out to the woman who'd been listed as Luke's mother. Another birth certificate for a baby born nearly fifty years ago. A little girl. Her death certificate was right behind it.

"It also looks like Laurel had another child," he said.

"She never mentioned that, either." She reached for the death certificate, her hands shaking. "Poor Laurel. So many secrets."

"Some of them even more upsetting." He held up a Polaroid photo of a woman, her face battered—eye black, lip swollen.

"Laurel," Virginia murmured, taking the photo from his hand. "She always said her husband was the best thing that had ever happened to her."

"Maybe she believed that, but there are several more. Dated." He handed her one that showed the same woman, blue and black smudges on her neck, eye blackened, lip cracked and bleeding. Someone had beaten her black-and-blue, and someone else had shot the Polaroid documenting the abuse that had happened decades ago. "She was keeping record of the abuse. Maybe she'd planned to go to the police."

"Maybe." She studied the photo, her eyes dark with

sadness. "I believed her when she said her husband was a wonderful guy. She showed me all the things he'd bought her and told me dozens of stories about vacations and spa days and flowers for no reason."

"Flowers as apologies. Gifts to say 'I'm sorry,'" he said without thinking, and she winced, obviously familiar with the pattern, with the thought process that allowed an intelligent, independent woman to be pulled into an abusive relationship. "When did he die?" he asked, changing the subject because he hated to see the darkness in her eyes.

"When Kevin was ten. He had a stroke." She worried her lower lip, lifted another Polaroid photo from the stack he was holding. "She stayed in this house, told everyone what a wonderful marriage she'd had, made the lies bigger and brighter, made the past so much more beautiful than it was."

"Maybe it was the only way she could survive," he said gently, and she nodded, the gesture stiff.

"Maybe so." Her shoulders slumped, and she glanced around the room. "No wonder she called this the blue room. She had a lot of sadness stored in that safe."

"I'm sorry," he said, sitting beside her, his fingers playing in the ends of her silky hair. She had beautiful hair, beautiful skin, the kind of soft prettiness that would only grow more lovely with age.

He could imagine her at fifty, sixty, seventy, could imagine himself, still looking in her face, still seeing her quiet determination, her strength.

"Me, too. If she'd been more open about her past, Kevin might have learned from the mistakes of his grandfather, or I might have learned from hers. But... she wasn't, and it's all water under the bridge. There's nothing that anyone can do about any of it."

"You're wrong there," he said. "He's part of the past,

and a big part of the present, and there is most definitely something that can be done about him. He can be tossed back in jail. You're certain Kevin never mentioned him?"

"Positive."

"Do you think he knew? Or maybe the better question is—do you think Laurel told him?"

"Based on all the other secrets she kept, I'd say she didn't. Laurel liked things tidy and nice. The idea of her son having an illegitimate child was probably difficult to swallow. Finding out he'd had two? I don't think she'd want anyone to know that. That doesn't mean Kevin didn't know. He kept secrets, too. I guess it was a family heritage." She smiled, but there was no humor in it.

Samson stood, growling quietly as he paced to the window and stood on his haunches, looking out into the yard.

"What is it, boy?" John stood and took a step toward the window, calling for the dog to heel. He didn't want Samson anywhere near the window if the suspect was outside. They knew Luke was armed, they knew he was dangerous. They knew he wouldn't hesitate to kill if he had the chance.

Samson retreated, still barking.

"Cease," John commanded, the sudden silence thick with something—tension, danger.

Downstairs, Dylan's dog sounded an alarm.

That was it. All John needed to hear. He called for backup, snagging Virginia's hand and pulling her into the hall.

Glass shattered. The blue room suddenly filled with smoke.

Something rolled across the floor skittering toward them as Samson howled.

"Get down," John shouted, tackling Virginia to the floor as the world exploded.

TEN

Chaos.

Dogs barking. Someone shouting. Darkness. Smoke.

Something nudged her cheek. A cold nose, a furry face.

Samson?

Virginia tried to get up, but John was pressing her down, his body a solid weight holding her in place.

"Wait," he said as she struggled to sit.

"The place could go up in flames."

"There's no fire. That was a smoke canister of some sort," he said. "He's just trying to draw us out."

"He's doing a good job of it," she said, pushing against John's chest. "I want out."

"We leave, and we'll walk right into the line of fire."

"We can't just—"

He pulled her to her feet. "*We* aren't going to do anything. Go in Laurel's room. Lock the door. Stay away from the windows."

He shouted the instructions as he dragged her down the hall. The smoke was nearly gone, just tiny wisps of it still swirling through the air.

"You're not going after him?" she said, fear making her voice hollow.

"I've been waiting for this chance for days." He opened the door and nudged her in. "I'm taking this guy down."

"What if he takes you down first?" she asked, all the old fears gone, all the nightmares disappearing in one moment of clarity—the past didn't matter, the pain didn't matter. The old hurts? They didn't matter, either.

All that mattered was John staying safe. All that mattered was him walking through the door again and again, smiling at her, telling her that she needed to be more optimistic. All that mattered was seeing where hope took them, seeing where trust led, seeing what the future would bring if she stopped being too afraid to grab hold of it, believe in it.

"Don't go," she said, grabbing his hand, trying to pull him into the room with her. "He's crazy. He could kill you and not blink an eye while he was doing it."

"I've got Samson, Dylan and his dog. We're better armed and better prepared than Luke."

"But—"

"I already called for help, Virginia. Backup will be here any minute.

"I—"

"Enough," he said quietly. "We're wasting time we don't have. You've got to trust me, Virginia. I know what I'm doing."

She looked into his eyes, had a million words she wanted to say. Only a few mattered, only a few could be the start of what they were going to build together.

"I do," she finally said, and he smiled, dropping a quick kiss to her lips.

"Stay away from the windows," he reminded her as he pulled the door closed, and then he was gone, and she was alone, fear pulsing through her veins, hope filling her heart.

* * *

Samson ran for the back staircase, barking ferociously. They hit the landing and raced into the kitchen. Dylan was there, Tico on his lead, lunging at the back door.

"He's out there," Dylan said grimly. "I caught a glimpse of him near the tree line at the back edge of the property. Too far for me to get a good shot, or I would have taken it."

"We get him now, or this could drag on forever. You stay here. I'll take Samson out."

"It's your show," Dylan said, his eyes trained on the back door. "I suggest you go out the front, though. The guy is probably packing."

No doubt about that. John was prepared, though. He knew what he was up against, knew that Gavin and Chase were only minutes away. Luke Miller was going to be sorry he'd come back. He was going to be sorry that he'd ever decided to make a play for Laurel's property.

That had to be what this was—an effort to get rid of Virginia so that Luke could inherit. It was a crazy plan, but Luke seemed like the kind of guy who just might think it would work. He'd been in and out of juvenile detention from the time he was thirteen until he was arrested at eighteen. Went to jail three times before he was put away long-term.

The guy had an inflated sense of his own abilities, and he seemed to think he could stay one step ahead of law enforcement.

It wasn't going to happen.

John opened the front door and eased outside. Samson was alert but relaxed, no sign that Luke was anywhere nearby.

"Find!" John commanded, and the German shepherd

rounded the side of the house. John hesitated at the corner, letting the dog get a good whiff of the air.

Nothing.

Had Luke retreated?

That would be the best-case scenario.

And the worst.

He wanted to take Luke down, put him in jail, make sure he never got out.

"Find," he urged Samson, and the dog trotted across the yard, then sprinted toward their old apartment.

Nothing was left of it but a pile of rubble.

They raced out onto the street. A dark car was parked a few houses up. Empty, but Samson spent a few minutes sniffing the door, scratching at the windows.

Luke's ride. It had to be.

That meant the suspect was still in the area, still trying to fulfill whatever mission he'd set for himself.

Kill Virginia?

Take something from the house?

Whatever it was, John planned to stop him.

He called in the location of the car, updated Gavin and Chase on his location and put Samson back on the scent. They moved toward the park, darkness pressing in on every side. No moonlight. The clouds were too heavy, the air thick with moisture. A few flakes of snow fell as Samson led the way through the empty park. Nothing moved. No animals. No people.

Behind them, a branch cracked, and Samson let out a long, low growl, turning sharply toward the sound.

"Come out of there!" John called, knowing the perp was close, that he was somewhere in the darkness of the trees. He stayed low, keeping foliage between him and whatever Samson could sense.

Samson growled again, his body tense, his scruff raised.

John reached for his lead, unhooking it from Samson's collar. "Come out, or I'll release my dog."

Nothing.

No movement.

No hint that someone was there.

Someone was. John felt the danger as clearly as he felt the cold air.

"I said—"

A flash of light cut off the words. Seconds later, he heard the gun's report. The bullet slammed into a tree a few yards from where they stood.

John released his hold on Samson's collar. The dog was well trained, he knew what to do. He needed no command, just leaped through the foliage, barreling toward the gunman.

Seconds later, Samson snarled, the sound a clear indication that he had the suspect in sight.

A man yelled, and the gun fired again, the bullet flying into the tree canopy.

Success.

John knew it, could hear the man's frantic cries for help.

He ran toward the sound, found Samson standing over the suspect, the guy's arm in his mouth.

"Release!" John commanded, pulling his gun, aiming it at the perp. "Don't move."

"I wasn't going to," the guy said, his face pale in the beam of John's flashlight, his eyes dark rather than hazel, his skin tan rather than light.

Black hair. A tattoo over his eye.

Not Luke Miller. This was a kid. Maybe nineteen. His gaze darted back and forth—his jerky movements and pockmarked skin telling a story of addiction that John didn't have time to read.

"Where's Miller?" he demanded, yanking the kid to his feet and frisking him. The gun he'd used lay a few feet away, and John cuffed the perp before retrieving it.

"I ain't talking."

"John!" Someone called, the sound reverberating through the darkness. Gavin. Chase was probably with him, both of them thinking they were chasing after Luke.

Which left Dylan alone at the house with Virginia.

He could handle himself, but John didn't like the feeling he was getting. The one that said he'd made a mistake, that he'd walked right into a trap set by a madman.

"Here!" he called, shoving the kid back the way they'd come.

"You're not taking me back to that house," he spat, struggling against John's hold.

"That's exactly where we're going."

"No way, man!" the kid whined. "I don't want to die."

That was it. All the words John needed to hear. Gavin was just a few feet ahead, Glory on lead, Chase a few yards behind. He shoved the kid their way.

"There's trouble back at Virginia's house," he said. "Call it in and take care of this kid."

"What kind of trouble?" Chase asked, moving in beside him as he raced back the way they'd come.

"I don't know, but—"

His voice trailed off.

Smoke was billowing up from somewhere just in front of them, the puffy tendrils of it dark against the clouds.

His heart raced, adrenaline pouring through him.

"Fire," he shouted, running back toward the house, his feet pounding on grass and then pavement, every nerve in his body screaming for him to hurry.

The trap had been set.

Send in a ringer, get one guard to leave the property, lure the other one out.

So much easier to take out one person than two, so much simpler to get to the person you wanted if you made her come to you.

If the house was on fire, Dylan would have to bring Virginia outside.

Luke was waiting there, ready to fire a shot as soon as they exited the building.

John knew it.

He tried to call Dylan, warn him, but his friend didn't pick up. Were there other officers nearby? Someone who could stop what was about to happen?

John couldn't count on it.

Please, God, let me get there in time.

The prayer filled his head, gave wings to his feet.

God, please, he prayed again as he raced out of the park and into the street beyond.

ELEVEN

Smoke filled the room, filled her lungs, the heat of the fire lapping at the floorboards making her want to open the window, climb out into the wintry cold.

She didn't. Couldn't.

She had to find Dylan, make sure he was okay.

She didn't hear his dog, didn't hear him, could hear nothing but the roar of the blaze that seemed to be sweeping up the exterior wall of the house.

A crack. A whoosh.

Heat. Flames.

All of it had happened too quickly for thought, too quickly for panic.

She felt the bedroom door—cool to the touch—and opened it.

There was less smoke in the hall, less heat.

"Dylan?" she called.

No response. She ran to the bathroom, grabbed a towel and soaked it.

She draped it over her head and shoulders, running for the back stairs.

No sign of the fire there. The house was eerily silent, the kitchen dark.

She crept into the room, cold air blowing in through the open door.

Someone was outside.

Waiting.

She could see the shadow of his head, the outline of his shoulders.

Not Dylan. This guy was too narrow, too short.

Not John, either.

She was terrified to move forward, terrified to go back.

"You may as well come out," someone called in a sing-song voice that made her skin crawl. "I've already taken care of your friend and his mutt. There's no one here to help you. It's just the two of us, so let's talk about what I want." A lie. She knew it. There was no way Dylan and Tico had been 'taken care of.' They were somewhere, waiting to step in. She just had to trust that they'd do it before Luke acted.

"What do you want?" she asked, her voice shaky.

She didn't move forward, didn't dare put herself within reach of Luke.

"Everything that belongs to me. All that is rightfully mine. This house. The money. All of it."

"The house you're burning down?" she asked, hoping to distract him, to keep him talking until help arrived.

And it would arrive.

She had to believe that, had to trust that John had realized what was happening and was heading back toward the house.

"Barely a flame, Ginny," Luke called in that same singsongy tone. "The wood and paint on this place are fire retardant. Laurel had a deep fear of flames. Didn't you know that?"

"No."

"I did. She told me all about it when she came to visit me in prison. Amazing what a little guilt will do. Opens up the floodgates, makes people reveal things they normally wouldn't. She told me that she'd had the whole place painted with something that would prevent a fire from taking hold. I checked into that before I came up with my plan. Just to make sure she was telling the truth."

"She didn't feel that guilty. She left the property to me," she said, purposely rocking the boat, purposely prodding him.

She needed to keep him talking, and she needed to keep him outside.

Could she get to the door? Close it before he had time to react?

"She felt plenty guilty," he growled. "But she felt guiltier about raising another wife beater. Third in the line, you know. The old man beat the stuffing out of my mom when she was pregnant with me. That's why they didn't marry. That's why I was born into poverty and squalor instead of excess. She should have just taken the beatings and let me have what was rightfully mine. It would have saved us all a lot of trouble."

"You're crazy."

"Am I?" He stepped into the kitchen, and her blood ran cold.

It was Kevin again, standing in the bedroom, the gun in hand.

You can't leave me. Won't leave me. Not now. Not ever.

She'd seen insanity in his eyes that day. She'd known she was going to die.

She saw it now, felt the same mind-numbing fear.

She had to act, but she didn't know which way to go, what way to turn.

"What do you want?" she managed to say.

"Your signature." He pulled a paper from his pocket,

the gun still pointed in her direction. "It says everything goes to me if you die."

"There's no way anyone will ever believe that."

"So?" He laughed. "It's the irony I want. You handing everything over to me right before you die. It's perfect justice."

"Even if you never get a penny?" She eased toward the kitchen counter, the knife block that was there. If she could grab one, she could defend herself.

"I don't want money. I want you to suffer like I've suffered. Simple as that, Ginny. You took my brother from me before I had time to really get to know him. You took my grandmother from me. You took my inheritance. My life. Everything that should have been mine."

"Nothing in this house is yours. It was Laurel's, and I had nothing to do with her death. I hadn't spoken to her in eight years when she died."

"She died from a broken heart. She lost everything. You did that to her."

"I didn't—"

"Shut up!" he screamed, rage contorting his face. She'd seen the same in Kevin's face too many times to count, and every time, she'd run from it, cowered from it, tried desperately to assuage it.

Not this time.

There was nowhere to go. Nothing she could do but fight.

She lunged forward, slamming into him as the pantry door flew open.

A dog snarled and snapped. A man shouted.

Feet pounded on the back deck.

She heard it all, felt the cold metal of a gun pressed to her temple.

"Stop!" Luke screamed, and the world went silent.

Not a sound from Dylan, who'd jumped out of the pantry and stood with his gun trained at Luke. Not a sound
from his K-9 partner.

"Don't do anything stupid, Miller," John barked.

He stood in the doorway, his firearm out, Samson
growling beside him.

A frozen tableau of men and dogs and insanity, the
gun still pressed to her temple.

"One move and she dies. You hear me?" Luke said.

She caught a glimpse of someone moving outside.

Chase or Gavin heading to the front of the house?

Probably, but they'd get there too late.

She could have told them that.

Could have told John that doing what Luke said wasn't
going to save her. She didn't say anything, though. Didn't
dare speak as Luke dragged her toward the hallway.

She thought she knew where they were heading. To
the front yard. To the spot where she'd collapsed. To the
place where Kevin had died.

Irony to die where her husband had killed himself.

She met John's eyes, saw determination there, knew
that he would risk everything to save her.

She couldn't let him die.

Couldn't let anyone else be hurt.

The gun was still there, pressed to her temple, the
metal cold and hard, but Luke was distracted, his grip
loosening as he tried to keep everyone under control.

This was going to be her only chance.

She had to take it.

She slammed her elbow into Luke's side, letting all
her weight fall against his arm.

Someone shouted. A gun exploded.

Pain seared her temple, stole her thoughts, and then
she was falling, Luke's laughter ringing in her ears, mix-

ing with memories of Kevin's voice, his shouts, his tears and moans and apologies, all of it there together, filling her head, pounding through her blood, carrying her away.

John tucked his revolver back into the holster, every cell in his body focused, every bit of who he was dedicated to one thing—keeping Virginia alive.

He'd seen the intention in her eyes a split second before she'd acted; he hadn't had time to tell her to stop, to wait, to let the plan play out—Chase and Gavin flanking Luke, taking him down from behind while John distracted him.

Only Virginia had acted first, and now she was lying on the ground, blood seeping from her head.

Luke lay a few feet away.

Dead.

John had taken the shot and had hit his target, taken him out with one bullet to the heart. He knew it. Couldn't find it in himself to feel more than rage for what Luke had done, what he'd been trying to do. The sorrow would come later. For the life that was lost, but not for the man who was gone. Luke had brought this on himself, and it had ended the way he'd wanted—with blood and death and violence.

John leaned over Virginia, Samson nosing in, trying to lick Virginia's cheek.

"Down," John said, pulling off his coat, pressing the sleeve to the seeping wound.

His hand was steady as he felt for her pulse, but his soul was shaking, everything in him shouting that he had to save her.

"Don't worry," she said, groggily, her eyes still closed. "It's just a flesh wound."

"This—" he said, wiping at the blood, relief coursing

through him. A millimeter in either direction and the bullet would have gone through the skull and into the brain, killing her almost instantly "—is more than a flesh wound."

"Probably," she responded, finally opening her eyes. "But I've always wanted to say that."

That made him smile.

She made him smile.

"I guess you've achieved your life goal, then," he said, applying pressure to the wound.

She winced, but didn't complain. "Luke?"

"Gone."

"I think I should be sorry for that," she said, her words slurred, her eyes hazy. She had a concussion at best. A fractured skull at worst.

She was alive, though, and that was something John would be forever thankful for.

"You will be one day. But not now. Not after everything that happened."

"Thanks for saving me," she said, as an ambulance crew moved in.

"You saved yourself, Virginia."

"No," she insisted, grabbing his hand when the paramedic tried to shoo him away. "You did. You made me believe in things I'd given up on. You made me hope for things I'd stopped believing I could have."

"What things?" he asked, brushing hair from her cheek, his heart aching with a love he'd never expected to feel. His life had been too busy, too devoted to his siblings, then his job. He hadn't had room for anything else until Virginia had come along.

She fit perfectly. In his life. His heart.

He wouldn't give that up.

Wouldn't turn away from it.

"Happy endings," she murmured, as the paramedics lifted her onto the gurney.

Her eyes were closed, but she clutched his hand, refusing to release him as they carried her out the back door.

She fell silent as they rounded the house, her hand going slack, her hold loosening.

He climbed into the ambulance, settled into a seat the paramedic indicated and nodded at Gavin, who was standing at the back of the ambulance, Samson on the lead beside him.

"I'll take him to my place," he said, and John nodded.

"I'll call as soon as I hear something."

"Trust me. That won't be necessary. Cassie is looking for someone to come sit with the kids. We'll be at the hospital as soon as she finds someone."

"No," Virginia mumbled. "That isn't necessary. Tell her to stay home."

"That would be like telling you to stop caring about your kids," Gavin responded gruffly. "Stay with her. Those are direct orders from Cassie," he said to John.

There was no need for the orders, because there was no way John was leaving Virginia's side.

The ambulance doors closed, and the vehicle raced toward the hospital. Virginia didn't speak, didn't moan, barely seemed to be breathing.

"Virginia?" he said, touching her cheek.

"I have a pretty bad headache, so this isn't the best time to talk," she responded.

"Too bad, I wanted to hear more about the things I helped you believe in."

"You just want to keep me awake, because you're afraid I'll lose consciousness and drift away for good," she accused.

"Guilty as charged," he said, and she opened her eyes and met his gaze, offering a soft smile.

"Don't worry, John. I'm not going anywhere." She reached out, touched his cheeks. "Not when I've finally found what I've spent my life looking for."

"What's that?"

"A place to belong. Someone to belong with. A chance for something that can last. I thought I had that with Kevin, but it was just a dream that I created. There was no substance to it."

"There will be plenty of substance to us," he promised, and her smile broadened.

"We'll see how you hold up under the pressure."

"What pressure?"

"Of Christmas shopping with a bunch of kids, of baking cookies with little people under your feet. Decorating with babies on your hip and a toddler whining for a candy cane. It's a busy month at All Our Kids, and I can't wait to get back to it." Her eyes drifted closed again, the smile falling away, a tinge of pink on her cheeks. "But I guess I'm getting ahead of myself. You'll probably be—"

"Doing all those things with you," he said, cutting her off, because he could see himself with her and the foster kids she worked with. He could picture Christmas in the house filled with children who needed more than gifts and treats. Who needed love, affection, constancy.

"Really?" She took his hand, lifted it to her mouth and kissed his knuckles. "Then you're a brave man, John. Much braver than I thought."

He laughed at that, squeezing her hand gently.

She had a long recovery ahead of her. He knew that, and he planned to be with her every step of the way. Through Christmas, the New Year, beyond. That was what commitment meant, it was what love meant, it was what he felt every time he looked into her eyes.

He wanted more of that. For himself. For her. He wanted to offer Virginia all the things she'd been searching for, all the things she deserved. Happiness. Joy. Security.

Love.

She seemed willing to ride things out, see where they led, what the two of them could create together. That was a beginning, and he thought it would also be an end—of walking the road alone, of forging his path without any commitments or obligations to anyone but himself. Just his job, his dog, his friends, his neighbors. No deep connections that could mold the heart and shape the soul.

He hadn't realized how much he'd longed for something more until God had set it in his life, shown him how much he was missing out on.

Snow was falling as the ambulance pulled into the hospital parking lot, heavy white flakes that coated the ground and seemed to bring a sense of renewal, of hope and of happiness.

Or maybe that's what Virginia had brought when she'd barreled into his life.

A perfect early Christmas present for both of them.

* * * * *

Dear Reader,

When I wrote *Protection Detail*, the first book in the Capitol K-9 Unit continuity, I was really taken with Virginia's character. I knew she had a story that needed to be told, and I was thrilled to have the opportunity to tell it. She's been through a lot of trauma, has faced a lot of trials, but she still has faith that things will be okay. As she faces her deepest fears, she learns that the darkest of times can lead to the biggest of blessings. I hope and pray that, whatever trials you face, you know the bounty of God's love and compassion for you.

I hope you enjoyed reading Virginia and John's story! I love hearing from readers. You can reach me at shirlee@shirleemccoy.com or visit me on Facebook or Twitter.

Blessings,

Shirlee McCoy

GUARDING ABIGAIL

Lenora Worth

To Shirlee McCoy, my friend and fellow writer.
Enjoyed being here with you.